The Only Road There Is

The Only Road There Is

Rebecca Bailey

Rebecca Bailey

Texas Review Press
Huntsville, Texas

FIRST EDITION, 2004

Requests for permission to reproduce material from this work should be sent to:

Permissions
Texas Review Press
English Department
Sam Houston State University
Huntsville, TX 77341-2146

Acknowledgments: My thanks to members of the writing community for their support, advice, and friendship: Mary Stewart, Carol Mauriello, M. Kay Miller, Nancy Sartor, the multitalented Joe Sartor, Marcia Ribble, and Gurney Norman; and to Nan Boone, who made the journey with me. I am grateful to the Kentucky Arts Council for an Al Smith Fellowship in Fiction, and to the Montana Artists Refuge in Basin, Montana, for the space and the excuse to make a trip west.

While the places in this story are real, the people, the establishments, and sometimes the roads winding through them exist only in the imagination.

Cover art by Joe Sartor.

Library of Congress Cataloging-in-Publication Data

Bailey, Rebecca.
  The only road there is / Rebecca Bailey.— 1st ed.
    p. cm.
  ISBN 1-881515-66-4 (alk. paper)
  1. West (U.S.)—Social life and customs—Fiction. I. Title.
  PS3552.A3738O55 2004
  813'.54—dc22

                                                    2004005820

To the Woo and to Tim

The Only Road There Is

—I—

THE FIRST AND LAST COUGAR DIVE

I am thinking that simplicity in life is the key to everything, and I am just thinking about things that I have with me in the car that I can get rid of—not throwing them away, mind you, but foisting them off on my unsuspecting relatives who never throw anything away and who will see my cast-off possessions as souvenirs of me rather than the materialistic put-downs they really are—when my mother announces that she's seen a sign for a Cougar Dive two miles ahead and that we probably should stop.

Six months ago the only Cougar Dive was virtual. My mother is eighty and she is an Internet junkie. She thinks she has a right to "electric," as she calls it, and that electric is as dependable as cold in winter and sunshine in June, and she's convinced she's discovered thousands and thousands of soul mates in chat rooms across the boundary-less land crisscrossed by the information highway. I have announced to her in every subtle and not-so-subtle way that I can think of that she's taken up residence in a la-la land more unreal than television, and that the United States Constitution gives her a right to freedom of religion and free speech, but I don't know of any government on this planet that gives its citizens the right to electricity, and that *virtual* means *almost* and not *computer*.

"You was never married to your daddy," she says in self-defense, and I do not bother to point out to her the foolishness of this statement since she says it after I have derided her about having soul mates whose legal names she does not even know. My daddy was a pure corn pone whose first name was General, and whose middle name was Dunn, and whose last name was Simpkins. At my birth I was given the name Brenda Marlene Simpkins, which I legally changed as soon as I got away from home to Starflower Jade-Eagle, but my mother still calls me Brenda, and Brenda Marlene when she's about had enough of me. Her name is Mauda Belle Adkins Simpkins, and we are in a car together and have been for several days, and I hope to be suffocated if I ever willingly stop at another Cougar Dive.

What is a Cougar Dive? You already know that the first one was virtual, and in my opinion the others aren't any better than that. It's a clearinghouse for products that aren't made anymore: any product line that's gone defunct, any color or flavor that's been discontinued. But at a Cougar Dive you don't buy just one of an item, you have to buy a whole case. One of my mother's virtual soul mates, Liz Taylor's Younger Twin, has bought cases and cases of Quisp and Quake and other suspiciously unavailable breakfast cereals. To my mother, this is the epitome of excitement.

My mother is after any kind of cosmetic bearing the brand name Our Lady of the Poppy. You remember the deep gold boxes and the fluid purple outline of the heavily-veiled and slightly pudgy vixen belly-dancing next to a camel in profile by a palm tree. Mom bought a case of the perfume early on, Dew of the Oasis, and she eagerly pried off the rusty lids of the deep purple bottles.

"It will have aged and mellowed," she predicted before inhaling, then coughing and blowing her nose in a panic. Now she is looking for lipstick: not just any lipstick but an Our Lady of the Poppy shade called Sultan's Kiss. "It's the exact color of a peony that's old enough for its petals to fall off," she explained. "I was wearing it when I met your father. General Dunn Simpkins," she added, as if I didn't know. I am older than forty and have never worn lipstick, even once, so you know I'm really wound up about this hunt for Sultan's Kiss.

"Another mile and seven-eighths," Mom says. I can't stand it. I simply can't. We have stopped at three Cougar Dives today, and I am so tired that it hurts when I try to straighten my fingers because they've been wrapped around the steering wheel for so long. I don't know how much daylight is left, but it's far more than I want. I'm too tired to think, but I try frantically to come up with something, anything, to distract the small BB of her mind from its relentless channel for at least two miles and one-eighth.

"Mom," I say, making my voice tremble just as the despised Cougar Dive sign comes into view. It is shaped like a giant *Z*, with a deranged-looking cougar atop the upper part, the shaft of the *Z* connecting the cougar to the water below, where gaping treasure chests await. I will not recount the derisive discussions I had had that day with my mother about what a wild and powerful cougar could possibly want with anything that would be in a sunken treasure chest—coins, jewels, wine, or cracked amphorae—and about how she called me a literalist and a Luddite and a grouch and a party-pooper. Remembering, I pretend to put on the brakes.

"Mom!" I repeat, trembly-voiced. "The brakes won't work!"

"Just let up on the gas," Mom says philosophically, "and pull her over easy."

Sometimes I have enough sense to know when I am beaten, to roll over and show my belly and slobber for mercy. This is one of those times. I give up. I let up on the gas and pull her over easy.

The gray gravel of the parking lot snaps beneath my tires. I pull to a stop as near the front door as I can get—there are a lot of cars here. I turn off the ignition and look at my mother. "Go on," I say, gesturing with my head. "I'm gonna sit in the car."

She purses her lips but doesn't say anything. Out of the car, Mom slams the door and hustles toward the Dive's entrance, which is cleverly designed to make patrons believe they are walking into a gigantic open treasure chest, the posts and lintels of the door painted a shocking metallic gold, clotted with a plethora of goose egg-sized faux rubies and sapphires. My small-boned hump-backed mother, trim in a loden green Fingerhut pants suit (a remnant of pre-Internet shopping), religiously sprayed silver hair, and teensy fake pearl clip-on earrings, vanishes inside.

I get out to stretch. It feels good to stand straight and raise my arms above my head. I shut the car door, locking it, and stroll around the parking lot. There are perhaps thirty-two cars, including mine, and I am tempted to count them. Don't be so anal, I scold myself, and observe that all the cars have out-of-state license plates. I realize then that I don't know what state I'm in. I could be in Utah or Montana or Nevada—there certainly are a lot of Nevada plates here. Maybe Texas or South Dakota. I don't care very much.

There is a sun in the sky above me, and my eyes are jumping around like bobbers in rough water. I have been driving too long, too many hours and too many days. No way will we make Dennis' by nightfall.

I decide I will walk all the way around the building. But around back, there's a generator, a dumpster full of flattened cardboard boxes, and a dripping faucet, rusted the same color as the poor bare ground trailing off toward the horizon. It spooks me. I feel like I've seen something nasty, and hurry back toward the civilized outpost of the parking lot.

There is a man standing looking at the back of my car, so I hustle over. The man is easily seven feet tall and his body is shaped like a green-striped cushaw. He's wearing a black cowboy hat, black slacks, black vest, and a blue chambray shirt with pond-sized sweat stains under the armpits. As I get closer I estimate that through the shoulders he's probably a thirty-eight but around the belly a fifty-two, and I sort of worry about him even though he's a stranger, because his feet seem dainty and elegant, frighteningly incapable of supporting and propelling this gargantuan specimen whose name must be Hector or Buster or Bronson. Now I see that hanging down the middle of his back is a long, heavy, carrot-orange braid, and I revise my speculation to decide that his name is more likely to be Percival or Bruce, or something self-conscious like Cedarwind or Sagegrass.

"Something wrong with my car?" I yell when I am within yelling distance. I trot over close enough to speak civilly or tackle him if necessary, but far enough away to lope off if he makes a grab for me.

"Nope. Just looking at your license plate. Not too many cars from the Bluegrass State in these parts." He continues staring at my plate, so fixedly that I'm suddenly spooked that he's memorizing the number for some nefarious purpose. "Carter," he says. "That a county?"

"Yeah. The only county in Kentucky with two state parks, Carter Caves and Grayson Lake. I live in Olive Hill."

"Olive Hill, Kentucky. Home of Tom T. Hall," he drawls admiringly. "I love little baby ducks." This refers to a line from a Tom T. Hall song. "Ever met him?"

"No. He doesn't live there anymore. Where you from?" I ask, not that I care but he's beginning to worry me, staring at my poor car like he's hungry.

"Paragould, Arkansas," he says expansively, and finally turns to look at me. His face is placid and benign, yet suddenly I've become reminded of the thin line upon which we always wobble. Sometimes I think about it when I drive, the mere yard separating the two vehicles whizzing along in opposite directions on a two-lane road, and the thin line is three feet and four hands. Or you're eating and something goes down the wrong way and you cough it up instead of choking. The thin line is a glistening wet inch and two lungs full of air. Now this seven-foot Arkansan is inspecting my license plate in the parking lot of some shithole a hundred miles from the Continental Divide, and could easily pull out a gun and shoot me or poke me in the eyes with his fingers or punch me in the stomach so that when I double over he karate chops my spine, shattering it.

"I was there once on my way to somewhere else," I say. "I figured you for a Kentucky boy."

"Once upon a time," he says, then he looks at me like I was a license plate. "What's your name?"

I have run this through my head before he's aspirated the last syllable. "Starflower Jade-Eagle," I tell him, because it isn't my name anymore.

"Dandelion Poopy-Chicken!" he shouts. "I knew it!" and he picks me up and swings me around so that I feel seasick when my feet hit the ground again.

"Obviously you know my brother—" I begin.

He is laughing. "Good ole Dennis Simpkins. It's been a long time. A long time. I'm Randolph Redfern."

"Doff Bloodplant," I say, remembering. "You were the one that dared Dennis to eat forty-five erasers in study hall in the eighth grade."

"And he's the one that et 'em!" Doff laughs gleefully.

"Didn't y'all have a sister that got—"

"Are you on vacation?" I interrupt, and we make predictable small talk about jobs and marriages and do you remember, and I am relieved when an equally tall female specimen breezes up and puts her hand on his arm. He introduces her as Helen, his lawfully wedded spouse, and I am even more relieved when they get in their Arkansas car ("The Natural State," the license plate brags) and head off in the direction from which Mom and I have just come.

I am staring at my own license plate, lost in thought and having completely vacated my brain, when I hear my mother call out, "Brenda Marlene! Look!"

She is beaming. She is radiant. She is carrying two boxes about the size shotgun shells come in. They are gold with the familiar purple logo.

"I got it! I got it! Sultan's Kiss!" she exults, shaking one of the boxes, and I cheer. She's babbling about which aisle she went down and which table she looked under as we re-situate ourselves inside the car. Carefully she opens the box and extracts one tube of lipstick. "The other is a fuchsia-red called Harem Heartbeat, but this is the one. This is Sultan's Kiss." She uncaps the vibrantly purple tube and twists it up. The lipstick is indeed the exact color of the petals of a nearly dead flower.

"I'm happy for you," I say. Mom flawlessly crayons her mouth as I slide back onto the highway, heading west.

—II—

CODY, WYOMING,
AND THE SCENIC WAPITI VALLEY

I am thinking that simplicity in life is the key to everything, and I am thinking just about things that I have with me in the car that I can get rid of, like the plastic bag on the floorboard of the backseat, full of Styrofoam coffee cups, wrappers from fast-food sandwiches, and tissues blown with snot from a thousand states but from only four nose holes, and my bag of filthy clothes, which suddenly seem more trouble than they're worth to get clean, when Mom says, "Are we there yet?"

"There where?"

"Don't be difficult, child. I'm tired. Where are we?"

"Here."

"Brenda Marlene," she warns. I wonder if in her heart of hearts that she thinks I'm gonna sit still and let her give me a whoopin'.

"We should make Dennis' place sometime tomorrow."

"Well, start looking for a motel. I'm feeling frail."

Frail. Horse doo-doo. That's what she says when she wants to take advantage of being old, when things have become tiresome and she wants a time-out. It means do what I want right now or I will whine, whine, whine. She got the Sultan's Kiss, so now it's time to go to Napper's House. If I "make" her stay awake too long, she'll do Bambi-eyes (yes, eighty-year-olds can still do Bambi-eyes) and pout and say, "Brenda Marlene, you're so mean to me," and do her best to squeeze out a pitiful aquamarine tear.

Well, she can squeeze out as many of the little jewels as she wants because I'll be looking at the endless ribbon of highway and not into the passenger seat.

"What direction are we going?" I ask her, thinking she might tell me what state we're in. I don't want to ask a thing like that.

"North," she replies promptly.

"How do you know that?" We're not, we're heading dead west.

"Because on a map north is always at the top and that's how we're going—toward the top. That's always the direction I'm headed: straight ahead. I don't look back."

"So how do I go east?" I ask, appalled that I can actually see the "logic" in what she's saying. She told me once that none of us actually go anywhere, that we all have separate personal identical planets that we rotate with feet or wheels, spinning our planet beneath us to move it around so that we get where we want to go. She also says that $2 + 2 = 22$. I get that, too.

"You just turn the map so that whatever direction you want to go is at the top," she informs me.

After a pause I say, "What was the name of that last town we passed through?" Surely I can get my mother to tell me where we are. I have to be smarter than she is.

"Greybull," she says promptly. She pronounces it *Gray Bull*, but the locals pronounce it *Grable*. It's like in Kentucky you don't say *Versigh*, you say *Versales*. It's one of the many things that make people think that Kentuckians are as dumb as rocks, but it seems to me that Kentuckians are smarter than the French, who put all those *L*s in there and then are too snooty to pronounce them. What a waste.

We are in Wyoming. (I knew that all along.)

"My home's in Wyoming, my hair needs a-combing," I sing.

"Pull over soon," my mother says quickly. "You're gonna soon start hallucinating that you can hit other cars and knock them off the road without scratching the paint on this thing. And when you close your eyes tonight and try to go to sleep, in your mind's eye you will see the road and you'll be driving, driving, driving."

"Thank *you*, Mom," I say.

"But it won't be like a real road," she continues. "Sometimes the road will be straight and deserted, sometimes it will be mountainous and deserted, but it will always be deserted. There'll be nobody but you. And if you cut the wheel hard enough, you can make curves happen, purple curves with puffy lips like clams. But it won't be like that Roger Zelazny novel where you can change the landscape through the powers of your own mind." I must be near collapse and having auditory hallucinations. My mother can't be saying all these crazy things.

She pulls down the visor. "There's no mirror," she says, looking at me.

"You're beautiful, Mom. You don't need a mirror."

"Don't sass me, Brenda Marlene."

"If you hold your head the right way, you can probably see your reflection in the window."

"I told you not to sass me. I don't *want* to hold my head the right way."

With great difficulty I leave that alone, and we are quiet for a while. I look at my watch. It is close to four-thirty in the afternoon. There is a lot of daylight left, but I am getting tired. I'm hungry, too. I see a sign—we are close to Cody.

"We should be able to spend the night in Cody, Mom."

"I don't want to stay in Cody."

She is quiet in such a way that I know she wants me to ask why. I don't care why. I don't care if she's allergic to a dust microbe that lives nowhere else on the face of this earth except Cody, Wyoming, and it makes her esophagus constrict so that she can't swallow and she drools all the time. Of course, it doesn't matter whether I say anything or not. She tells me anyway.

"I had a bad dream about sleeping there. I thought I laid down on the softest bed I ever put my body on, but the longer I laid there, the more I was sure that there was something under the mattress right underneath the base of my spine, right where my tailbone is. I finally got up, and I could see because of a nightlight shaped like a mermaid. I raised up the mattress and there was a bloody pistol under it. I picked it up, and fighting snakes fell out of its barrel."

"You didn't bring that pistol with you, did you?" I ask, too sharply.

"Then it turned into one of those dreams when I wanted to run and I couldn't. It was like my feet had been set in cement. I strained and strained so much that I was soaked with sweat when I woke up. I thought I might have a heart attack just from the memory of it."

"We'll at least have something to eat there." I don't tell her that we'll sleep there too, because I remember the map. There ain't a blessed thing between Cody and Yellowstone National Park but a scenic highway named Wapiti. And I don't want to sleep in Yellowstone. I've been there before, and it smells like hell. Don't walk on the ground, just the boardwalks, they tell you. They don't tell you how often that seething ground eats the boardwalks, and I hadn't bothered to ask. I just walked fast.

More cars now, and buildings. We are Somewhere. My foot feels heavier on the gas, and I think of fast food, and salivate.

"Slow down a little and let me put on some lipstick."

I want to argue, but I don't. I slow down. It saves trouble. She uncaps the precious Sultan's Kiss and embarks on a delicate, exact application while I rubberneck for fast food joints. Salty french fries might be all that save me. I have a sixth sense for ferreting out junk food, which, I must confess, is pathetically easy in twenty-first-century USA. I remember when it was harder. Much harder. Then I really did need the nose to sniff out the boiling grease in which innumerable bits of meat and vegetable had been fried and hopefully left dripping. Now everywhere there is one franchise or three or six, and we make our selection based on condiments applied to our hamburgers. The thrill of the hunt has certainly diminished.

I pull into the fast-food oasis I've chosen for us for tonight, not that they're much different from one another. "Do they have baked potatoes here?" Mom asks.

Of course not, so I pull out and pull in again a block down the street.

"Let's eat in the car," Mom says. And my whole life flashes before my eyes.

Boyle County, Kentucky, 1967. We don't live here, but have gone to visit Mom's sister Stella who does. We are leaving, headed home toward Morgan County, a long drive. My father, General Dunn Simpkins, gives in to a rare impulse and takes us to a hamburger joint in Danville. We all go in. Dennis is eight, and is such an appalling slob—Dennis was an enthusiastic eater who ate with both hands for years—that someone looks at us! My mother never gets over it. We were in a restaurant, and someone looked at us. Excuse me while I collapse from shame. Even now that Dennis is grown and has not lived with her for going on a quarter of a century, the fear is still there: that someone will look at her in a restaurant.

"No, let's go in," I say. "I'm tired of sitting—"

"You'd have to sit in there, too."

"—in this car. I want to sit with my legs straight out and be able to stretch my arms."

She doesn't say anything. I turn off the car.

I open the car door and get out. So does she.

We choose a table. Mom will sit there while I order the food and then bring it. She tells me she wants a cheeseburger and ice water, so I bring her that and a baked potato, too. I have a chicken salad, an extra-large order of fries, and a medium-sized clear carbonated beverage. As I walk back to the table, I see that she is making fish lips.

I put the tray on the table and parcel out the food. "What's this?" she says, pointing at the baked potato.

"A baked potato," I say, never too proud to state the obvious.

"I didn't ask for one."

"Yes, you did."

"I did not."

"When we pulled in at the other restaurant."

"All I did was ask a question. I didn't say I wanted anything."

"Well, want it or not, you got one."

She unwraps her cheeseburger and bites at it daintily. She is a slow eater. I will have eaten everything I bought for myself by the time she eats half her sandwich. I am stabbing happily at my salad when I notice that Mom is acting weird, weird even for her. She is looking at the occupants of the table next to ours, three aggressively outdoorsy men, probably in their thirties, and she is making fish lips at them. I roll my eyes, having realized what she's doing, when one of the men looks at me with a question in his eyes, like "What's wrong with her?" or "Shouldn't she be on a leash?"

"New lipstick," I mouth at him slowly behind Mom's back, and swipe around my lips with a fry like I'm putting some on. A swift kind smile illuminates his whole face.

I can tell he's about to do something. Will he elbow his companion and point out the beautiful woman at the next table? Will he look at her and say, "Whoa! Nice lipstick!"? Will he snicker rudely? Pretend he didn't understand? Roll his eyes?

The next time Mom glances his way and simpers, he does the grandest thing he could possibly do—he winks at her.

And Mom, God love her, winks right back.

Thereafter she behaves herself, and we leave the restaurant and I find a motel. We will sleep the sleep of the smugly prosperous, and head out early the next morning toward the barely crusted-over seething sulfur pool known as Yellowstone National Park.

LEST WE FORGET THE SCENIC WAPITI VALLEY

What about the scenic Wapiti Valley? In our motel room is an endless stack of tourist information about Cody, specifically about (duh) Buffalo Bill Cody, who single-handedly slaughtered enough buffalo to account for about three-quarters of their eventual near-extinction. From what I am reading, he exploited the Indians in a nicer way than most, and paid them very well for it. I also learn that "wapiti" is an Indian word for "elk." And that the scenic Wapiti Valley is so gol-darned beautiful that seeing it I'll be in danger of fainting, because I will be so light-headed with delight that I will simply keel over.

Buffalo bullpoopy. We believe all this, and the next morning actually wait until full daylight to leave so that we can be sure to see it all. It is not the most direct route to our destination, but we figure another hour in the car will be a small price to pay if we're wending through paradise.

"Where is it?" Mom asks after we have borne about as much of this beauty as we can deal with and still retain our nominal sanity. "Where is the scenic? Where is the wapiti?"

The valley is easy. We are in it, on it, mucked up in it practically to the axles, but my filthy blue car keeps its wheels a-rolling. None of the full-color exclamatory brochures bothered to let us know that this fall the scenic had been dug up so the road could be rerouted and repaved. The Cody Tourism Board and maybe the whole state of Wyoming will hate me, but this is the ugliest stretch of godforsaken highway I've ever traveled in my life. The mud is the color of semisweet chocolate or upchucked raisins, and it allows us to speed along at thirty-five miles per hour, thirty-seven on a straight stretch, because there are lots of sharp turns.

On and on we slug. "There's a good reason for us not seeing any wapiti," I say to Mom.

"I know," she says. She's wearing Harem Heartbeat this morning, and has just about pursed it off. "They've got enough sense to keep the hell away from here."

A few minutes later she says, "Brenda, do you have any idea how much coffee I drank this morning?"

"There's no place for me to stop," I say. "Not a rock or a tree to hide behind."

"I don't know why Dennis didn't stay home in Kentucky like a good boy," she mumbles for the nine hundredth time on this trip.

"Me neither, Mom," I say, hitting a pothole. We both squeeze our sphincters.

The day is beginning to warm, and I roll down the window. Mom doesn't bother to protest—she knows that our molasses-slow speed won't begin to muss a single strand of her fiercely helmeted hair. The mud gloops like heat from an old volcano. I feel like I am driving through a landscape of endless diarrhea, like I'm in a fairy tale and a spell has been put on me so that I am small enough to fit into a Matchbox car, and a naughty toad of a boy has thrown me into the depths of an ogre's outhouse. The infernal depths of a very old outhouse belonging to a very sick ogre.

I find I'm less and less aware of Mom's gentle moans of discomfort because I have Zenned out, zoned out, into a state of numb transcendence. I am borne on a translucent wave of pink equanimity. My thoughts vanish, but if I had still been having thoughts they would have been very, very clear. The sun is bright. The air smells like morning. I do not have to go to the bathroom. I will see my brother this afternoon. All things must pass. I wouldn't describe myself as happy, but I am undeniably at peace with my place in the world.

Until there is a sound like a rocket being launched beneath my car. "Brenda Marlene!" my mother chides, as if this were all my fault. Actually it's hers. If she hadn't had Dennis all those years ago, we wouldn't be here.

"Hush, Mom," I say. "Let me drive."

It becomes increasingly difficult. I have to find a place to pull over. Up ahead I see a spot with some gravel where gargantuan landscape-destruction machines have been parked. I chug along slower and slower, and pull over, turn off the ignition, and hop out.

"Oh, thank you," Mom breathes. "I thought you'd never stop. I'm gonna go pee behind that bulldozer." I am not paying much attention because I am staring at the front tire on my side. It is as flat as flat can be. At least I'm reasonably sure I haven't damaged the rim. This ground has the sponginess of box springs.

It's like this: I have a spare tire in the trunk, a real spare, not one of those temporary tires that look like a motorcycle wheel. I'll have to unload all our luggage to get at it, but it's there. I also know how to change a tire. But I have weenie arms. It will take me untold hours to get the lug bolts off, and I will likely flay my hands and fingers in the process.

I am still staring at the tire, waiting for a lightbulb to go off in my head, when my mother hurries back. "Ready to go?" she asks brightly.

"The tire," I say.

"I know. Cleanliness is next to godliness, they say, but we can wash the car later. I'm sure Dennis has water—"

"Mom, the tire's flat."

"Well, shit," she says with finality.

We stand there in the bottom of the ogre's outhouse. I sigh and open the trunk. I might as well act like I know what I am doing. With the trunk open—it's a hatchback—I can toss our luggage directly into the backseat. It's too muddy to set it out on the ground.

A car passes. Someone honks and waves. Mom waves back.

By the time the next car comes along, I have the spare out in front of the car and the front end jacked up. Mom is in a snit because I won't let her sit in the car while it's on the jack. She is telling me for the ninth time that her knees hurt and she needs to sit down. My equanimity has vanished so that I have counted how many times she has said this. If she says it one more time

I'm gonna hand her the lug wrench and tell her to make herself useful.

The next car stops. Two guys dressed in Star Trek outfits get out and walk toward me. They both have on the blue pajama-top shirt of Mr. Spock, and now I can see that they are Chinese. They are both as skinny as straws.

"Break down?" one asks.

"Flat tire," I say.

"We can fix," the same one says, while the other one grins. They look like twins. Knights in shining armor cleverly masquerading as Oriental adolescent Vulcans.

I begin to explain about the lug bolts, but the one who does all the talking says, "Is okay, lady. We know." So they go to work. Mom and I stand and watch.

"My name is Shyue," says the talking one. "Pronounce like *shit* but without the *T*. My friend is Ansel." He pauses to adjust something, and that quickly they have the flat tire off. Ansel rolls the good tire toward the wheel bucket or whatever it's called, the place where the tire goes. "I want to know why Ansel chooses the American nickname that sounds like 'asshole.'" Shyue shakes with silent laughter while Ansel just grins. I'm sure Ansel has heard this many times before.

"Ansel is a fine name," says my mother.

"I think so, too," says Ansel.

"There's someone else in your car," I say. I am about to introduce myself, though I am not sure which of my names to use, but then I forget.

"Is girl," says Shyue. "Cindy. She is scare of dark. Scare of cold too."

"It's not dark or cold now," I observe.

"Cindy is sleeping," Ansel says. They are almost finished with my tire.

"Where are you boys from?" my mother asks.

"Ohio," Shyue says. "Is a very small place. We study the ESL in there."

"You know this place?" Ansel asks, grinning.

"No, no. I mean your home country."

"Taiwan, ROC," Ansel replies.

"China?" Mom asks.

"No," says Shyue. "Not Chinese. We are Taiwanese." He shakes his head. "China is a very dirty country. Dirty." He stands up and hands me my lug wrench. "We have finish."

"I don't know how to thank you," I begin.

"Is okay. Is no problem," Ansel says, smiling with friendliness. "We are glad to help you."

"MAY WE PAY YOU MONEY?" Mom asks very loudly, like they will understand better. As far as I can tell, they understand everything just fine.

They shake their heads. "No," says Shyue. "We are having fun in America. We drive very fast. Roads very straight and there are no cars in here. Not like Taipei. When cop stops me for ticket, I say, 'No English. No English.'" Again he shakes with silent laughter.

"Wait," says Mom. She reaches into the backseat. She hands a purple tube to Ansel. "For Cindy."

"I will give to her. She will very like."

Shyue nods. "Is girl," he says again.

"Thank you again," I say. "I don't know what I would have done without you."

"No problem," Ansel repeats.

"Have a safe trip," I say. "And a happy trip."

They bow, which embarrasses me immensely. I blush.

"Bye-bye!" they say, waving and heading toward their car.

When Shyue puts his hand on his own car door, I shout, "Live long and prosper!"

Their perpetual grins broaden and they flash me the well-known Vulcan hand greeting. Then they are gone.

My meditation has done me good, as has the kindness of strangers, and the rest of the trip is not so bad. Soon I begin to see buildings, a sign advertising a ranch that takes in boarders, a stray café, a billboard reminding me of where the nearest Indian casino is or where I can buy tourist t-shirts at incredibly low prices. This Scenic Wapiti Valley drive has to be coming to an end.

We still have the car windows down. Mom wrinkles her nose. "What's that smell? Is the car overheating?"

"No, Mom!" I exclaim. "That's the sulfur of Yellowstone National Park!"

In a few minutes we pass through the park's east entrance, where we buy a pass good for ten days. The road is still bad but gradually improving, so that by the time we reach Tower Junction it looks like a real highway. Mom is itching to stop and take a picture.

"Let's go on to Dennis's," I say, making a right turn, to head us back east. "We'll come back and be tourists another day, before we go back home." She's not happy with me, but I'm driving and she can't stop me.

In a half-hour we are in Montana, in Cooke City, which is our destination.

Sort of.

—IV—

DENNIS ISHMAN SIMPKINS

Dennis Ishman Simpkins. That's his name. My baby brother, who had so blithely corrupted my beloved Starflower Jade-Eagle into Dandelion Poopy-Chicken. Who was as big as a mountain, sly as a fox, wily as a bear, clever as a well-educated coyote, and as aromatic as a herd of male buffalo in summer. In short, he considered himself a Mountain Man, in capital letters.

Dennis and I have always had trouble with our identities and our names. I guess the trouble was that both of us were blood hillbillies, and knew it and hated it. All you had to do was look at our faces or hear our names, and you knew. Our hair was no particular color—neither were our skins nor our eyes. We had both et squirrel and stripped tobacco. As children, we both had jammies made of floweredy feed sacks. There: I've done used a hillbilly word—*floweredy*. It was all too guttural and unenlightened for me, too tame and civilized for him. I longed for incense, incantations, and a harp. He grubbed out ginseng and goldenseal roots to sell for money to buy a bowie knife. "Brenda" is a name for a hairdresser. "Dennis" is a name for a librarian. Our father told us to wish in one hand and spit in the other and see which got full first.

It was my experience that neither of them ever filled, ever.

Cooke City, Montana, is less like a city than anything I have ever seen in my life. Its road is a slice through a mountain, a big mountain, with ramshackle board-and-batten buildings and walkways made of planks. Surely to God there's a hitching post somewhere and a drooling old bay nag tied to it. I would bet real money that none of these buildings has insulation, and that in winter the wind whips through them, slinging snow through cracks a finger wide.

"Is this for a movie?" Mom says in awe. "I'd like to be in a movie."

That quick we have passed through the town. I pull onto the narrow shoulder and make a U-turn. There is, of course, no other soul in sight on the road.

"Brenda Marlene, you have just broken the law," guess-who scolds. "I need to put on some lipstick before we get to Dennis'. I'm liable to scare him otherwise."

"I'm scared right now. I missed my turn somehow, and don't be worrying me about lipstick or I might drive off the side of this mountain."

"You just do that, and I'll get out and drive. You act like it's so hard."

But I see a practically invisible rut veer off behind one of the buildings, and I decide that this is a road. It has more switchbacks than I can count, so I stop counting after eight. Maybe this is a road for snowmobiles. It certainly wasn't made for a navy-blue sedan housing two old women and twenty-three tubes of lipstick. Oops. More than that—Mom surely had five or six tubes already in her purse before she hit the jackpot.

I guess it really doesn't take as long as it seems like it's taking. We go up and up and up. We have rolled up the car windows because now the air is uncomfortably cool in the nostrils. Mom has managed to kiss herself with the lipstick. My elbows and hands ache because the road's ruts have repeatedly jarred the tires and the steering wheel in directions I'm not interested in them going. Mom tells me she needs to go to the bathroom, and I reassure her that we'll be there soon. Personally I am not so sure, and am considering making a solemn vow to never drive off the blacktop again when the road, such as it is, stops. Cleverly, I put on the brakes and also stop the car.

"Don't tell me we have another flat," Mom snaps.

"I think we have to turn around and go back," I say slowly.

"That's ridiculous. Go on."

"Do you see any road? I don't."

"Well, that never stopped your father, General Dunn Simpkins. He said he could drive anywhere the timber's been cut."

"If the timber's been cut, it means there's a road." I put on the emergency brake and turn off the ignition. "I'm going to get out and look around. Are you coming?" She decides she will get out for a minute and stretch her legs, but that she will wait by the car.

It does feel good to stand up. The air is cool, and I reach into the backseat for a long-sleeved shirt. Its buttery yellow color makes me feel more competent once I have it on, plus its warmth feels good. It must be a good twenty degrees cooler here than it was down at Yellowstone.

Off to the left there's a trail, probably a deer trail—no, not a deer trail, a wapiti trail (or a moose trail or a bear trail)—and I follow it. The rocks are nice, though I have no idea what they are. The same for the trees and the plants of the undergrowth. I hear some birds. The sound is pleasant, but I don't know what they are either. A naturalist I ain't, but I'm thinking about the food chain, and that out here I might not be at the top of it. I decide I would rather know how it feels to be killed by a bear than to know how it feels to be *et* by one.

I whistle tunelessly, hoping it's not an elegy or a dirge. Or bait.

I don't walk very far before I see some kind of shelter that was obviously constructed by a human. I wouldn't go so far as to call it a house, but there are logs and some large rectangles of flat tin flung together with a general stab at ninety-degree angles. I don't know what the Unibomber's hut looked like, but this must be its kissing cousin. A chill comes over me that has nothing to do with the altitude. I am sure that this is where Dennis lives.

"Dennis?" I call out, as quietly as I can while still making a noise. This place spooks me.

I edge around the building's perimeter, squawking out tentatively another couple of times. I have no urge to peer inside the opening that surely is the door, for if I were a grizzly that's exactly where I'd go when I wanted to hide.

"Dennis?" I bleat out one more time, and then fairly run back to the car.

Mom is talking to a giant: *Dennis.*

"Howdy!" I shout out, trotting the rest of the way to the car. "Guess you thought we'd never get here!"

"Well, Poo," he says, "are you growed up yet?"

We shake hands because in our family we never hug, and make predictable small talk about how are you, it's been a long time.

He looks strange, even for Dennis. He'd never dressed like he fell out of the pages of *GQ*, but now he looks like he's scrounged his clothes out of a dumpster that had been set on fire, and then the fire was beaten out with a really muddy shovel. He always bought his clothes second-hand, and maybe there'd been quite a run on old trapper pants and flannel shirts at the Cooke City rag sales. I back away from him as soon as we've shaken hands because he smells like a dead fish.

He has his head shaved, too, which throws me for a loop because he's always been as determinedly hirsute as a chimp, with long kinky brown hair billowing around his head like weeds. He has a ratty ZZ Top beard down to his waist, and he's wearing reflective sunglasses.

"Nice shades," I say, tapping my fingers on the mirrored lenses. He doesn't flinch. "Where'd you get 'em, steal 'em from a tourist?"

"I'm a man of means by no means," he drawls, and I wonder when he started listening to Roger Miller. I guess I'd heard "King of the Road" on *Hee-Haw*, but Dennis never watched TV, even as a kid. I don't know what he did, probably sat around practicing how to say "varmint" so he sounded like a cowboy rather than a hillbilly.

"What are you calling yourself now?" he asks me.

"Cerise Cloudmist," I say.

Mom snorts. "I don't know why Brenda Marlene isn't good enough for you."

Because it was good enough for *you*, I think. "You can call me Rissy," I tell him.

While Mom continues: "Now, Dennis, he's always been such a good boy." She simpers and makes fish lips at him. He is oblivious to her lipstick. "Called himself Dennis his whole life."

I ask about the hovel I've seen in the woods—it is indeed his, and Mom worries aloud whether he has indoor plumbing. I wonder if he's even got a pee bucket, but I keep my mouth shut.

"Don't worry, Mommy," he says in a pandering tone. "I'm gonna take better care of you than that. I won't make you stay there."

I'm thinking I don't even want her to see that pile of boards when he says, "I bet you girls are tired and hungry. Let's go back into town and I'll treat y'all to the best burger this side of the Rocky Mountains."

"It has been a long time since breakfast," Mom allows, simpering again. Here I've taken care of her my entire life and Dennis hasn't even spoken to her for thirteen years, yet she's never once simpered for me. I want to slap her.

"You got a car, or do you want to ride with us?" I ask, praying he's got a clunker somewhere. Even with the windows down, I wouldn't get his smell out of my car in a month.

"Naw," Dennis says. "I'll drive myself. I'm parked over there where I can turn around." He gestures back down the mountain, and I see a sludge-green pickup parked in some weeds off to the right. He gets in his vehicle and we get in ours, and twist and jostle our way back to Cooke City.

He parks behind the buildings we drove in front of less than an hour earlier, and I pull to a stop beside him. Mom has asked me about a hundred times what Dennis has on the grille of his truck, and I answer about twenty-seven times before I realize the question is rhetorical.

"Ask him yourself," I grouch, getting out of the car and slamming the door.

"Don't think I won't," she says, getting out on the other side, and also slamming the door.

We join Dennis. He has put on a hat. The hat looks about forty years old and as though it has been sat upon many times, but still it is a vast improvement over the bristles poking out of the skin stretched across his lumpy skull.

"Honey, I want to ask you a question."

"Go right ahead."

"She wants to know what's on the front of your grille," I

butt in. I know Mom wants to say—*Brenda Marlene, what's gotten into you?*—but she doesn't because she's really trying to make Dennis like her.

"What's it look like?" he counters.

It's some kind of skull, we can easily see that, but for some reason neither of us says anything. Mom laughs awkwardly.

"Buffalo skull," he says.

"That's gross," I say.

"It's natural," he says.

"The hell it is," I exclaim. "There's nothing natural about an animal's head bolted to a piece of metal attached to a gasoline-powered internal combustion engine. Poor old buffalo."

"I'm a buffalo warrior," he says, looking at me.

"You're a glow-in-the-dark white man with a belly the color of a maggot—" I begin, but Mom interrupts.

"I think it is very nice," she says insincerely but emphatically. "Very nice."

"Let's go eat," my brother says.

We follow him to something that looks like a shed. A hand-lettered sign above the door reads MOOSE LICK CAFÉ. We enter.

Inside it's very dark. There are no windows, just a single forty-watt bulb glowing in the ceiling light, but a candle burns on every table. In less than a minute, I can see round tables covered with red gingham tablecloths, and on each table is a clear glass with some pieces of live greenery in it.

"This is nice," Mom says as he takes her elbow to lead us to a table. I'm amazed that I agree.

When we are seated, Dennis points toward a chalkboard that serves as the menu. He recommends the Teddyburger. "It's named for Teddy Roosevelt," he says before I can ask. "He's a hero in these parts."

"Is that why you look so much like him?" I say.

We agree to have Teddyburgers, and he goes to the bar to order. He returns with forks, real napkins, Pepsis for us, and a Rolling Rock for himself.

"Cheers," I say, and we clink our bottles together. I am feeling that this is probably the most ridiculous thing I have ever done in a lifetime filled with ridiculous moments. I want to go home. I'm tired. I don't want to think about lipsticks, switchbacks, or state lines for a long, long time. This place is so suddenly alien that I feel panic rising like black bile in my throat.

Mom elbows me. "Let's go to the bathroom."

I nod, and we pass behind the bar to the ladies' room. The wooden door latches with a peg. It is a one-seater. I turn my back so Mom can go first. I feel a draft from the right-hand wall, and, sure enough, there's a gap between the boards big enough to slide my hand through. I stoop and peep into the crack, and see our vehicles simmering in the afternoon sun.

"Brenda Marlene, are you looking into the men's room? I'm ashamed of you," comes my mother's querulous scold.

"Don't be ridiculous," I snap, standing up. "It's just the outside."

"I'll wait and let you flush," she says.

While I take my turn, she washes her hands before getting out the Harem Heartbeat. "Let me give you one of these," she says, sliding a purple tube into my purse. "You might need it sometime."

"Okay," I say. "Thanks."

She puts on her mouth, then says, "Dennis has changed."

"You ain't just whistling Dixie," I agree.

"He has not smiled one single time. It's like he's sitting on barbed wire." She sighs. "When I saw that sign 'café,' I was hoping this would be an Internet café, too. I haven't been able to tell a single soul about my find of the century. My lipstick."

"You told me. I'm a single soul."

"You wouldn't be if you was married. Tee-hee." She thinks this is funny.

We go back to the table and are gobbling our Teddyburgers—they are fantastic—when I remember Doff Bloodplant.

"I didn't tell you, Mom," I say, pausing to wipe my mouth, "I saw Randolph Redfern in the parking lot while you were in the Cougar Dive."

"Well, Lord have mercy. What's he up to?"

"About seven feet." I can't keep from making the dumb joke. "He lives in Arkansas. You remember Randolph Redfern? He asked about you," I say to Dennis.

"Old Randy. How is that son of a gun?"

I don't know what to say, because this man sitting with us has just proven that he is not my brother. I think I have been suspecting this. Randolph was never Randy, always Doff. Doff and Dennis were best buddies for all of middle school and high school, until Doff and his family moved off. Dennis never called anybody by a regular name or nickname if he could think of something else. I was *Blender* before I was *Dandelion*. It was why I told him he could call me *Rissy*—I knew he'd never say *Cerise* and had no idea what he'd trash it into.

This Dennis is an impostor. I roll this over in my head again and I hear Mom, as if from a great distance, asking about the nearest Cougar Dive.

—V—

PLEASE REMEMBER THAT THIS IS NOT A SPY MOVIE

When our Teddyburgers are about gone, not-Dennis goes back to the bar and returns carrying a tray with three cups of steaming coffee and three slices of pie. "Mulberry," he says. "A local delicacy." I eat it gingerly, wondering if he knows anything since he obviously doesn't know who he is. I suspect it is strawberry-rhubarb, but I eat it because it is good. So is the coffee. The food here is something else. You think at a place like this they'd serve gray rags or pulverized moose teeth.

"Well, girls," not-Dennis says as we finish up, "I got a night job guarding at a place up at Red Lodge, so what I'm gonna do is take you somewhere to spend the night since my place ain't fit for man nor beast, and it especially ain't fit for womenfolk." He guffaws. "It's up toward Gardiner, a nice little Victorian bed and breakfast. Soft beds and flowery wallpaper. You'll be comfortable there."

"That sounds lovely, dear," Mom says. "We don't want to be any trouble."

"No trouble at all. My treat." He pays and we go outside.

"We'll follow you," I say, "but tell me how to get there just in case we lose you."

"You won't lose me—"

"You don't know your sister's driving," Mom interrupts. So he gives me some directions, not very enthusiastically, but they don't sound very complicated. After all, there's only one paved road out here. I just stay on it and don't hook a left at the intersections that go back into the park, though the road that we'll take will go through the northern part of Yellowstone—it's the only road there is.

"I'll be slow because I don't know the roads."

"You'll be okay. Just stay on the blacktop."

"Gotcha," I say, and we finally separate to get into our own cars. Mom gets in and immediately locks her door.

I start the car. Dennis pulls out, and I wait, fiddling with the seat belt and the visor until three cars have passed, and then I pull out.

"That ain't Dennis," I say, deciding to hell with subtlety.

"I know," Mom says quickly.

"When did you figure it out?"

"There's something that just ain't right about him—"

"He called Randolph Redfern *Randy*. That's crazy." I drive along at forty, forty-five. The buffalo-skull truck is not too far ahead. "We are not following him to no damn Victorian bed and breakfast."

"Why not?" Mom asks.

"Why should we? We don't even know who that person is. Is it some loony who's having a psychotic episode and hallucinating that he's Dennis, or is it some criminal luring us along for some nefarious purpose?"

"Nobody would want *us* for any nefarious purpose."

"He's got to be either a lunatic or a criminal. I vote for criminal. I'm not going anywhere he wants me to go."

"But I'm tired and want to lay down for a while."

"Mom!" I can't believe this. "Forget it! It's just jumping into the fire." There are still three cars between us, and this is not a straight road. We are almost immediately back into Yellowstone National Park, and the closer we get to Tower Junction the more traffic there is. Thank God. "I know good and well I talked to the actual Dennis two nights ago because I told him that I'd seen Michelle Kitchen and he called her Rec Room. Whatever happened has happened between then and now. What I want to know is where our Dennis is and whether he's okay."

"You're right, Brenda," Mom says soberly. "We can't go with him."

We are quiet for a few minutes, then I say, "Can you reach into the backseat?"

"I think so."

"Good. Get into your suitcase and change your clothes."

I can tell that she is looking at me like I am crazy. "So he can't hunt us down by what we are wearing." She looks down at her loden-green pantsuit. She reaches back into one of the bags, and extracts a baggy denim dress that belongs to me. She very slowly unbuttons its front buttons and slides it around the outfit she's wearing like it is a jacket. Then she slides the other things off underneath it.

Meanwhile I am wondering what I can do. Ditching the butter-yellow flannel shirt and putting on a hat is the best I can come up with quickly. We arrive at the turnoff for Tower Junction. I go past it.

"That's it?" Mom says incredulously. "That's your plan? We change clothes?"

"The next junction will be into Mammoth Hot Springs. We're going to slip away from him there." I am driving slowly enough that four cars have passed me. Two of them have also passed the buffalo-skull truck. "There are lots and lots of tourists there. Lots of cars. Once he realizes we're not behind him, it'll be too hard for him to find us."

"There's no traffic out here," she says.

"You got a better plan?" I say. "Follow him to where he wants us to go and take a nap? There'll be plenty of people at Mammoth Hot Springs. There's a resort motel and restaurants and shops and everything. It doesn't look like it's got any business being in a national park. It looks like some place back east for socialites."

"He knows what this car looks like. He's probably memorized our license plate number. He's probably bugged the car."

"He's not been alone with the car."

"When we were in the ladies' room."

"Nope. I looked outside, remember? I could see the car. Nobody was out there."

"So what do we do when we get to Mammoth Hot Springs?"

"We get something to eat and we call the police."

Mom snorts. "The police. What would the police do?"

"We'll file a missing persons report on Dennis. They can

go to the bed-and-breakfast in Gardiner and catch the impostor, and make him tell us where Dennis is."

"The police will just think we're crazy."

"The police work for us," I say stubbornly.

"You got a lot of learning to do, girl," she says, shaking her head. "And why do you want to eat? We just finished eating a meal big enough to founder us."

"We want to be in a public place—"

She snorts again. "You think Dennis is going to kidnap us or mow us down?"

Mow us down. God save us from television. "Don't call him Dennis. That person is not Dennis."

We are quiet for a few more minutes. We are just frightened enough to get angry with each other, and I don't want to argue with her. I want her to do what I want her to do, and I want her to be quiet about it.

"This is it," I say a few minutes later. "We lose him here." I drive slowly enough to time it so that I am at the junction of Mammoth Hot Springs just as he goes around a curve and we are out of his line of vision. "Hold on." I make a sharp left.

Almost immediately we are in a swarm of humanity. There are people on foot crossing the road, and traffic is moving slowly, inching along. Soon I see why: At the clinic a herd of elk has decided to take a siesta, under the trees and on the porch, and the tourists are all stopping to take pictures of them.

"Those aren't horses, are they?" Mom asks, squirming in her seat to look at them.

"Nope. Those are elk."

"Wapiti!" she exclaims happily. "These are the wapiti from the scenic valley. They're so pretty! This trip has been worth it after all! Where's the camera?"

"Not now. We'll come back later, I promise." I feel guilty. Just because I've seen all this doesn't mean that she has. But I'm in such a hurry to lose myself and my car in all these people. I think of that truck with the obscene buffalo skull on the grille, and I'm positive that man has a shotgun on the seat right beside him. "We're escaping," I remind her.

"I know. But I'd love to pet one of those," Mom says wistfully.

"I promise we'll come back here," I say again.

"They have the prettiest little butts. That lighter hair around their tails looks just like a heart."

It looks just like a target to me, but I keep my mouth shut for once. Right now I have a great deal of sympathy for targets.

The traffic finally moves past the peaceful wapiti, and I see the resort hotel. I pull off the main road to lose my filthy vehicle among all the other cars.

"What's this?" Mom asks.

"It's a motel," I say. "We'll spend the night here."

"We will not. We can't afford a place like this."

"You're right, but you said you needed to lay down—"

"Not for fifty dollars a minute, I don't."

"Okay." I sigh. "Let's go in and call the police."

"The police won't pay no more mind to you than if you was a tadpole."

"Humor me." I back into a parking space. "Let's go."

She sighs, but goes in with me. The police are mechanically polite, and they say they will check Dennis' cabin and place of employment, but are skeptical when I tell them my impostor theory. They tell us to find a motel and stay there a couple of days, then call them back. They suggest we go south to Jackson. If we are in danger, we'll be farther away, plus there will be lots of people there, too. I give the policeman a description of the man passing himself off as Dennis and of his truck. There is no license plate.

"Figgers," the policeman says. "Half the people out here think the laws apply to everybody except them."

Jackson. I don't want to go to Jackson. Jackson Hole must be a hundred miles away. Mom says she can make it, and we get back in the car and back on the road. The policeman has suggested that I drive to Inspiration Point and then down along the western boundary of Yellowstone Lake to West Thumb, and then the John D. Rockefeller Memorial Highway will take us through the Grand Teton Park into Jackson. We are both quiet. I have no idea what Mom is thinking about, but I vacillate between worrying about what has happened to the real Dennis and stewing about what we'll have to pay for a motel room at a tony playground for the rich like Jackson Hole.

I drive and drive. I am tired. Northwestern Wyoming just goes on and on and on. I have driven a long way today to get nowhere. I want to go home. Maybe I will go home. But it's a long way to Kentucky—I won't make it tonight.

Yet when I at long last get to Jackson, I am so tired that all I want to do is not be in a car for a couple of hours. I look for a Motel 6 and can't find one, so I check in to some chain that seems familiar. I feel a great sense of relief when we are in our room with the door bolted behind us.

Mom collapses on the bed. I don't feel much better. It's nearly 7 p.m.

I wash my face in cold water, then put on some clean clothes—I feel like I've been wearing the same outfit my entire life. When I come back into the main room, Mom is still flopped out on the bed.

"Are you awake?" I ask quietly.

"Barely," she mumbles.

"Stay right there. I'm going to go get some food. Don't let anyone in."

"Food sounds good."

I go to a grocery store and buy peanut butter, bread, some fruit, chips, and juice. Then I go to McDonald's for some regular hot grease and salt for supper, including a giant coffee. When I get back, Mom is sitting at the little desk leafing through the telephone book.

"I'm looking for movie stars' names," she announces.

"Good luck," I say, and laugh. She's beginning to look human again. All this riding in the car is bad for her. It's bad for me.

She doesn't quarrel about what I've brought, and we eat slowly and without speaking, glad to relax. When the food is gone, I tell her what I'm going to do, and, more specifically, what *she* is going to do. She is going to stay in the room, eat the food I've brought, and if I'm not back in twenty-four hours she will call the police. She agrees, and I shove some money and my driver's license into my jeans pockets. I give her a quick wave, and I'm gone.

I'm going to find Dennis.

—VI—

I DON'T KNOW WHAT HAPPENS NEXT

I know exactly where I am going—I am going to sneak back to the place in Gardiner that not-Dennis gave me directions to. Where, for whatever devious reason, he wanted me and Mom to go.

Not-Dennis. Already I'm tired of not having anything to call that ugly jugheaded lump of human protoplasm. But I don't want to call him Jughead—there's something too affectionate and indulgent about that. I know: I'll call him Bristlehead.

It is dark, and I have to be careful with my driving. I'm not driving through Tower Junction and Mammoth Hot Springs again. I am sick of Yellowstone—it's such an enormous, alien place. Instead, I pick up a new route in Jackson and soon cross into Idaho.

I am sorely tempted to break the law, to pull over into some dark parking area and switch license plates with a lone, stationary vehicle. But my Kentucky license plate is so mud-spattered that it's a proper camouflage the way it is, yet I am so tempted . . . but it would be more trouble than it's worth in the long run. I am always so tempted to do bad things. And I confess: I enjoy it. I truly enjoy being tempted, and I do enjoy succumbing to temptation. The good God is all-forgiving, right? Which, in itself, is another temptation . . . .

I wish I were somewhere else. I wish I were in Manhattan, Miami, Massachusetts, Minnesota, Michigan, anywhere except here crossing into Montana again. But this, too, is futile, unproductive thinking. I must be a machine. I must be an automaton. I must be an imbecile. I must be a good sister.

I wish I were adopted. I wish Dennis wasn't my brother. I wish Mom wasn't my mother. I wish I wasn't related to any Simpkins on the face of the earth. But I don't have to go to anyone's rescue. I can get on the interstate and head back east. Dennis doesn't need me, us—he's done without us entirely for thirteen years. And the woman I call Mom can just live in Jackson. Surely there are some old women there she can go shopping and drink coffee and gossip with. I'm not like anybody else in that family of ignorant hillbillies, that bunch of card-carrying frequenters of yard sales and recipients of government commodities. I hate cheese. I have always hated cheese. That commodity cheese was just a dried-out block of half rotted milk. *Ewh!*

So I'm not obligated, right?

I can't hear you. Right?

One souldeep sigh can fill the entire void of an all-but-empty mechanized shell in the middle of nowhere so that it reverberates for uncomfortable minutes. Remember that, okay? You don't have to learn it for yourself.

My head falls and I drop the wheel. The car lurches, jolting me full awake. My heart pounds like I have been running, being chased. Lord, I fell asleep at the wheel. I could have killed myself. I don't know what to think, so I don't think. I have to find a place to pull over, I think crazily. I'm nearly panting with retroactive fear. I have to find a place and pull over so I can calm down. Surely there's a café or something. I feel like I'm going to be sick.

Someplace where I can pull over and stop the car, and roll down the window and just breathe the cool night air for a minute or two, to refresh myself, wake myself up . . . .

My hands are slick on the steering wheel. Surely I haven't driven the twenty miles I feel like I've already driven since . . . .

There. Ahead on the left. It must be a casino, all those lights.

It's a Cougar Dive. I pull in anyway and—

I am somewhere, and I am awake. I am still partly in a dream, and Peter Gabriel is singing me that song about "red rain is falling down all over me," but it isn't me and it isn't Peter

Gabriel. I am something curly and blonde and I am wearing pants that are as tight as duct tape, but it is still me. Gabriel isn't anything but a voice, maybe the voice of God serenading me from somewhere and suddenly I know I have to run, but I can't. I have to untape myself out of my pants first—they are red and so beautiful—and I can't use my hands because my nails have just been polished with 24K gold and diamond dust, and they aren't dry yet. My nail polish is worth about $6,000 and I can't escape until my polish dries and it will never dry. I just stand there, my knees soldered together and my hands up in the air, fingers delicately parted, nails glinting and sparkling. And Peter Gabriel won't rescue me despite his heavenly name, because he is distant and invisible. I am awake and I am dreaming and I can see the monster that is coming to get me . . . .

"*Waugh!*" I yell to wake myself and jerk to sit up straight, but I am already sitting up, the seat belt cutting into the soft round meat of my shoulder. Quickly I roll down the window, sure I am about to vomit. The mountain air is cool, too cool in my nostrils, but it wakes me up and clears my head, and I inhale deep lungfuls of it until my queasiness has passed and I feel awake. The sickness of the bad dream is still somewhere at the back of my skull, but the more my heartbeat slows down, the farther away the dream goes. Soon there is no hope of calling it back, and gladly I let it go.

I'd managed to get to the side of the Cougar Dive before I fell asleep. I push the button on my little Indiglo watch and see that it is nearly three-fifteen in the morning. I sigh. The curse of the Simpkins women is upon me. I have to go to the bathroom.

I wait six minutes, and not a single car passes. As quickly as I can, I open the door, get out, shut the door, run around back and go to the bathroom, then tiptoe to peek around the front of the building. Yes, that bright red glow . . . a Coke machine! Salvation is at hand! My dad used to call pops and pop machines "sum-bits," swearing without actually committing the sin of uttering the correct syllabication, but this one looks to me like the Holy Mother Angel of Mercy. But I don't have any quarters.

Wait! I'm living in the twenty-first century, right? Machines can take a dollar bill and spit back change, and I do have some bills with me. I snitch one out and walk boldly right into the light and get myself a pop. Then I run back to the car, holding the door open just long enough for the light to show me that no one has crept in and lies crouching in the backseat, then I jump in, slam the door shut, and lock it. My heart goes nuts again but calms quickly—I rub the cold red can across my forehead before I pop the top and chug the first sweet, fizzly sip.

"Amen," I say out loud. "Amen."

As I pull onto the road, I am thinking that I have finally simplified my life. There is nothing in my car except my tools, me, and what I'm wearing on my person. How sleek and streamlined my life has become.

I make Gardiner around 4 a.m. I go where Bristlehead has told me to go. As I suspected, it is no bed-and-breakfast. A damaged neon light that looks like it's been through a tornado blinks ineptly in a pale lime green: K VI 'S M TEL. The parking area is small and steep. I have pulled in and turned off the ignition before I realize that in the parking lot is a battered pickup truck with a buffalo skull leering from the grille.

K VI 'S M TEL

Right this minute there is nothing in the universe darker than the eye sockets of that buffalo skull on the cowboy truck. But before I can think, the passenger door of my car opens and Bristlehead gets in.

He grabs hold of my wrist before I can get my door open.

"Poo!" he hisses. "Where have you been? I've been worried sick. And where's Mom?"

"Mom," I spit. "She's not your mother. And who are you anyway? What have you done with my brother?"

"God, Poo, don't be an idiot."

"Why is that skull on your truck? It's obscene."

He sighs, and relaxes his grasp on my wrist just a little. "It's part of my cover."

"Your cover?" I exclaim in amazement. "Are you a cop? Are you protecting Dennis?"

"I'm not a cop—"

"You're not Dennis!"

"Why do you think I'm not Dennis?"

"Because you don't have any hair! Because you never smile! Because you don't know Randolph Redfern's right nickname!" I shout, feeling exceedingly stupid.

"It has been thirteen years since we've seen each other. Why do you expect me to be identical to the person you thought I was thirteen years ago? If you don't change, you die. So I've changed. Deal with it. Are you the same as you were thirteen years ago?"

I don't say anything.

"Of course you're not. You don't even have the same name,

Cerise. Your hair's a different color. You've gained weight. So maybe you're not my sister."

I still don't say anything. He relaxes his grip on my wrist, and I jump for the door.

"Doff Bloodplant!" he shouts.

I slump back into my seat. "What were Jeff Bailey's nicknames?" I ask. I had previously thought up a bunch of questions to ask the impostor. Or the real Dennis, when I found him.

"House, Barn, Silo, Outhouse, Inhouse," he says tiredly.

"What song was playing at my senior prom when you threw up in the punch?"

"'It Don't Come Easy.' Ringo."

"How many sisters does Mom have?"

He sighs. "Stella Belle, Liza Belle, Lillie Belle, Ruby Belle."

"Who did Ruby Belle marry?"

"Russell James. We called him Toadman. Their two kids are Cathy and Danny. Danny got killed in Vietnam."

"What did I major in in college?"

"I don't know and I don't give a damn. Cut the crap, Poo. Where's Mom?"

I look at him. I can't see much of him in the dark.

"Why did you cut your hair off?" I ask.

"It's part of my cover—"

"Your skull is really ugly."

Again he sighs. This is an unexpected, old-womanish way my brother has changed, all this sighing.

"Okay," I say. "What's going on?"

"Let's go in. It's a better place to talk. It's safe," he adds, a comment which serves to increase my uneasi-ness.

I reluctantly get out of the car and follow him through the steep, dark parking lot to the back of the building. I'm thinking that if he prefaces anything with, "You're not going to believe this, but—" I'm gonna kick him twice in the shins and run like hell. Then as we are approaching the door, I think that if he knocks using a secret code, before the door opens I will crush a rock into that ugly, ugly skull of his and run. I don't like this guy. I don't trust him. But when he simply opens the door and enters, I follow him.

He closes the door behind me, and flips a wall switch. Two table lamps glow dimly. The lamp shades are covered with small brown feathers. That makes me even more scared and out of sorts than I already am. The room smells musty, like an old drawer full of bobbins that were wound forty years ago. More than that—forty years ago was only 1963. More like 1933. Bobbins wound on treadle sewing machines. On the walls are Hudson Bay blankets, framed etchings of ugly buildings in Europe, and whole skins of ring-necked pheasants, feathers intact.

I feel like I'm suffocating.

"You want anything to eat or drink?" Dennis asks.

"Ice cream," I say promptly, knowing it's insane.

"We don't have any ice cream," he replies, as though what I've just said is rational. "We'll have ice cream and candles when the truck gets here tomorrow afternoon. How about a piece of red velvet cake instead?"

"Okay." I realize that I have to be dreaming. Real life couldn't possibly be this foolish, this non-coincidental. I will think about taking off my shoes and tanning the tops of my feet in spring. I will remember the time I waded in the ocean in Hawaii, wearing a red and white lei around my neck and a sky-blue silk dress long enough to get wet in the spume, and how it unromantically felt like toilet paper plastered around my ankles. I will think about hot onion rings—anything except all these things that are so obviously wrong, like feathers on a lampshade.

"Have a seat," he says. "I'll bring it to you."

I nod and sink into an upholstered purple Victorian armchair. Historic Montana dust rises around me. I figure I'm sleeping, so I jerk my arms and legs and stand up as fast as I can. Nothing happens except that more dust rises.

Dennis comes back—I might as well give up and call him Dennis—and hands me a plate. The plate has a crack running through the center. It advertises Wells Fargo. On it is about a quarter of a red velvet cake with caramel-pecan icing. A bright green plastic fork is stuck down into the middle of it. He hands me a glass of water, and I accept that, too. I cannot believe that I am actually going to eat this cake, but I am actually going to eat it. I realize that I have never before eaten in a dream, and I feel unnerved again.

Dennis sits on a couch across from me. He also has water and a gargantuan slice of cake.

"Why are you undercover?" I ask.

"In the eyes of the government I am a criminal."

"And in your own eyes?"

"In my eyes I am a good son of our Earth Mother."

"What'd you do?"

"Blew up a bunch of snowmobiles in Yellowstone last winter. Gonna blow up some more this winter, too."

"How'd you do that?" I feel like I'm watching television. The cake is good.

"Poo, you don't wanna know." He shrugs. "I was seen, sorta, but I didn't leave no evidence. It's why I cut my hair and grew a beard, and put that skull on my truck. Trying to blend in with those militia people. The cops leave them alone, and don't do nothing but persecute the environmentalists." He inserts about a quarter-cup of cake into his mouth and still manages to chew.

"You took up monkeywrenching," I say.

"Took it up decades ago," he says with his mouth full. "Don't aim to stop." He swallows, then peers at me. "You ever heard a snowmobile?"

I shake my head *No*.

"It sounds like somebody ripping up gristle, the gristle of a giant or a god. If the sky was a piece of paper and somebody tore it in two—that's what a snowmobile sounds like."

"I'm not arguing with you. They're toys for rich lazy people."

"Not all of them. Some people would be snowed in all winter if they didn't have a snowmobile to get around in. But snowmobiles got no business being used in the parks. It scares the animals and it ain't natural. They don't have any defense against that."

I am eating like I've never tasted food in my life. "So why do the cops care?" I ask when my mouth is empty.

"Blew up six of their snowmobiles," he says with a guffaw. "Some kind of cop reunion or picnic or something. Big men out there spooking the buffalo and the elk." He snorts disdainfully, not easy with a mouthful of red velvet cake.

"I told the cops in Yellowstone that you were an impostor who'd kidnapped my brother."

"That ought to freak 'em good. What'd you tell 'em?"

I tell him. He sighs again. "I guess they went and trashed my cabin again."

"That place was already trashed—"

"Where's Mom?"

It was my turn to sigh. "She's in a motel in Jackson."

"Wyoming?"

"No, Kentucky. Of course Wyoming. Because the cops told us to go there," I say to the next question he's bound to ask.

"Whose name did you check in under?"

"Mine."

He looks at me.

"Cerise Cloudmist. It's my legal name. It's what's on my credit card."

Again he sighs. What is it with the sighing? "She ought to be okay then. If you'd checked in under Simpkins, maybe the cops might goof with her. You slept any tonight?"

I shake my head.

"There's a room fixed for you upstairs. Rest for two or three hours, and then we'll go get her. Or maybe we'll all stay in Jackson and do our visiting there. Teton's nice. What do you say?"

I am tired. I nod, thank him for the cake, and follow him upstairs.

He opens a door for me, and I walk in ahead of him. "Welcome to Kivic's Motel," he says with a laugh.

"What's that mean?"

"Kivic's Motel? It's what this place used to be called. Never heard of the name 'Kivic' before. The man that owns it now, his name's Wiggins and he lives up in Missoula. His grandson lives here. We got to snooping in the attic one day and found receipts and stuff from the 1920s and that old sign that Jimmy hung up outside. Probably you didn't see it. Jimmy'd like to find something that says that Teddy Roosevelt stayed here—"

"He's a hero in these parts," I say.

"—but so far he's not run across anything. I guess some of the first tourists who come to Yellowstone could have stayed here, though I don't think this ever was a big fancy place. You got any luggage or anything you want me to bring up?"

"Nope. I'm traveling light."

"Suits me." He's turned on another lamp—this one without feathers—and is showing me where I can go to the bathroom. "'Bout seven or eight," he's saying. "Let's make it eight. We'll have a good breakfast, and then drive down to the Hole and see Mom. Maybe we can do something touristy."

"Mom would like that," I say, and yawn. "She's always wanting me to stop so she can take pictures."

"Maybe she can take some this afternoon. Sleep tight."

"Thanks, Dennis," I say, but he has vanished.

The bed is big, and looks soft and clean. I turn it down, and I am afraid I check for bedbugs before I sit down on it. I don't find any. The room is actually pretty nice. The light is coming through a pale pink lampshade, and it looks like everything in the room is done up in various shades of pink and yellow, mostly florals. It does have a Victorian look, yet I'm sure that in the cold light of morning the windows will be grimy and if I looked I could find dustballs under the bed.

There is an armoire. I get it into my head that it's really a door and that someone will sneak in on me during the night, so I have to get up and open it. It's a computer armoire! So I boot it up and get into my e-mail, and send Mom a long message about what's going on. Despite the hour, she's probably on-line at this minute, writing purple prose to Liz Taylor's Younger Twin about her marvelous Cougar Dive finds and the terrors of being cooped up in an automobile with her daughter. After I send it, I think about it for a minute, then forward a copy to a friend at home, with some additional messages about what to do if there's an accident, because I still don't feel safe. I still don't know what's going on.

Then I shut everything down, wipe my fingerprints off, turn off the light, and climb in bed.

I am smothering.

I try to cough and my mouth is filled with feathers. I try to roll over, but I can't—something is on my chest. I flop out from under it. I'm not even awake, I'm dreaming, and instantly I'm sucked back into sleep.

It happens again.

This time I scream and jerk upward into a sitting position.

~42~

I switch on the light, and at the foot of the bed is the biggest cat I have ever seen. It must weigh twenty pounds and its head is as big around as a grapefruit. The cat stares at me, then opens its mouth, but no sound comes out.

"Hello, kitty," I say, holding out my hand, and the huge creature waltzes over and helps me pet him. Several times the cat meows but no sound comes out. He's purring like a lawn mower so that makes up for it. This is a sweet kitty.

I look at my watch—it is nearly twenty after seven. The room is so dark, surely daylight should be coming through the windows by now. I get up and pull back the curtains. There is no window! Just the regular old wall with its wallpaper. I smack it with the flat of my hand. Life just gets dumber and dumber. I want to go home. I need to start keeping a list of how many times I've thought that. Surely it's a record.

I sigh, and hope it's not catching (the sighing). I have to go to the bathroom. At least I don't have to get dressed first, since I slept in my clothes. I slip on my shoes, walk across the room, and grasp the doorknob. It turns but nothing happens. I rattle it, and try again, pushing hard. Nothing. The cat says, "Mrrrink."

That bristleheaded numbskull has locked me in.

I kick the door. "Let me out!" I roar. "I'll sue! Do you hear me?" The cat scampers beneath the bed.

Footsteps pound in the hallway. "Have you lost your mind? Pipe down," Dennis says on the other side of the door.

"You locked me in!" I scream.

The door opens inward. Dennis is standing there, the knob in his hand. "I was trying to open the door the other way," I say slowly.

He sighs. "Sometimes I think you ain't got any sense at all. Come on to breakfast since you're up. You seen Othello?"

"Who?"

"Big cat. Here kitty kitty! He likes to wake up company." The cat emerges from beneath the bed, hurries to us, and opens his mouth but makes no sound. "Master of the silent meow," Dennis says, picking up the big ole cat, who is happy to hang in Dennis' meaty arms. "This way," he says to me.

I make a stop at the bathroom, and then follow him

downstairs to a cramped kitchen with a wood cookstove and a yellow Formica table and chairs that look as though they have been through several floods. The room is comfortably warm. A tall skinny guy with dark hair that doesn't look like it's been combed in a week is flipping pancakes.

"This is my sister, Brenda," he says.

"Jimmy Wiggins," he says, and we shake hands.

"My name's not Brenda." Dennis pours me a cup of coffee. I can tell from the looks of it that it will taste like tar, but I know I will drink it because I really need some caffeine. The back of my skull feels like it's about to crack off. "Call me Rissy."

"What's he call you?" Jimmy asks, shrugging a shoulder at my brother.

"Poo," I say.

"I'll call you that, too. You both call me Jimmy, we both call you Poo." Unaccountably, Dennis laughs. "You ready for some pancakes, Poo?"

"Slap 'em down," I say, biting back the urge to inform him that civilized people don't eat until they've been up at least forty-five minutes. There is no doubt that I am not among civilized people. I include myself in that sweeping generalization. I have definitely gotten up on the wrong side of the bed, though it was the only possible side to get up on.

I sit down in an icky chair at the icky table. Dennis is still holding Othello, and he sits in another chair. Jimmy hands me a plate with three whole-wheat pancakes, beautiful with brown blisters and puddled with butter, and a green plastic fork stuck down in the center of them.

"Is this the same fork I had last night?" I ask. The cat works his nose in the general direction of my plate. I think the pancakes smell good, too. "Got any syrup?"

Dennis hands me a glass. "Homemade," he says.

"Cool." I pour some on my pancakes. "How'd you make it?"

"Boiling brown sugar and water till it gets thick. It ain't rocket science, but it works."

I am wondering if the coffee was boiled with brown sugar. It tastes like something that would come out of the oil pan of a tractor built in 1952. It tastes like gym socks boiled in swamp water. This ain't the kind of simplicity that I was yearning for. I ain't got nothing, but the nothing I've got ain't what I want and it's ugly to boot. I want to go home.

"Have you eaten?" I ask Dennis.

He nods. "I didn't go to bed, just dozed on the couch. Been up about an hour."

"How come you got a computer in the bedroom? I'm glad you do. I wrote Mom a letter last night and told her what was going on. She's got a laptop that she carries around everywhere so she can chat with her buddies about all the Cougar Dives she's made me stop at."

"My Mom loves those, too," says Jimmy. "They make me sick. What's she buying?"

"Lipstick. But not just any lipstick. Our Lady of the Poppy in a shade called Sultan's Kiss. She also bought some Harem Heartbeat. That's what she was wanting you to notice, Dennis, when she was making fish lips at you while we were eating. She was wanting you to tell her how pretty her lipstick was."

"Damnation," he says. "Why would I notice any blame fool thing like that?"

"My mom buys Star Trek stuff," Jimmy says, leaning against a cabinet and eating a plain pancake folded in half. He looks like the cartoon Moses in The Prince of Egypt.

"That's at least interesting," I say. "These pancakes are really good."

"Thanks. So your mom's into the Internet?"

I nod, chewing. "There's some chat room she really likes. She's found her soul mates there, or so she says."

"All the lonely people," Jimmy says. "Where do they all come from? Wise words from the Prophet McCartney."

He sits down at the table with us, with another plate of pancakes. The cat jumps down from Dennis' lap and pads over to sit by Jimmy's legs.

"You gonna eat them pancakes, Poo, or just admire them? It's a long way to Jackson," Dennis grouches.

"Be quiet. I know how far it is. I drove it last night," I grouch right back.

"Well, gimme your keys. I'll go start your car and it'll be warm and ready to go when you're finished."

That sounds okay by me, so I reach in my pocket for the keys and then toss them to him. He catches them, lurches up from the table, and disappears.

"He's weird," Jimmy says, pouring syrup from the glass onto his pancakes, "but I like him."

"He's different from what he used to be."

"How so?"

I shrug. "I guess he's just a grown-up now, and I've never known him that way. He doesn't smile as much. He seems meaner and more inflexible. I mean, he was always the way he is but he's just more so now." I take another bite and realize I hadn't said anything and hope that Jimmy hasn't noticed. "How long have you known my brother?"

"About six years. We used to night-watch at the same place. I quit when I moved here. I caretake this place for my granddad. Dennis's not lived here long, just since he got in trouble with the cops. They trashed his cabin."

"I saw it," I figure that's safe. I'm wondering if Jimmy blows up snowmobiles, too, when Dennis stomps back into the kitchen.

"Neither of the damn cars'll start," he growls. "Somebody took out the damn batteries."

"I did," says Jimmy. "They're in the mud room."

"What'd you do that for?" I ask as Dennis stomps off again.

"So nobody else would. It's happened before," he tells me.

I don't ask, but finish my pancakes quickly, then run upstairs to the bathroom to wash off a little before I go back in the bedroom and check the e-mail. I have a message from Mom—everything is okay, it's been nice to sit and catch up on her communications. Liz Taylor's Younger Twin has offered her $100 for a tube of Harem Heartbeat. For the first time I wonder what she paid for the whole box. I e-mail her that everything is okay, and that Dennis and I should be there sometime this morning and to be sure and stay away from the cops. I write this even though I know she will think *I Told You So.*

We say goodbye to Jimmy—"Live long and prosper!" he says—and we both get in my car. Dennis says he will hitchhike back or walk if he doesn't get a ride.

"I'll bring you back," I say.

"Nope," he says. "I don't want y'all to come back up this way. It ain't safe."

He's driving. "Is there a McDonald's anywhere near here? I need some more coffee."

"McDonald's is ruining the world," he starts.

"Spare me," I say. "I know all about the rain forest being destroyed so they can grow cows. They still make good coffee."

He is silent for a minute or two. He grudgingly says he knows of a place along the way, when he flips on the turn signal and suddenly says, "Got time for a detour to see Darlene?"

I burst into tears.

—VIII—

A LONG TIME AGO

I learned to breathe when I was fourteen. I don't think I ever considered it before then—I knew I did it, but it was just something that happened without my awareness, something even less deliberate than the way food usually appeared when I was hungry, how it got dark when I was sleepy. But it was when I was fourteen, my fourteenth birthday, to be exact, that I first went outside as far away from the house as I could get without noticing even a tingle of fear behind my knees, that I slowly drew in my breath. Determinedly I pressed my lips shut and instinctively opened my nostrils and, as slowly as I could, I breathed in. My ribs expanded and I braced my legs because I could feel the weight of it in my belly. I could feel the ground pulling me in, and it was calling my name. I didn't listen. I closed my eyes and held my breath until my nose began to go numb, and as slow as Christmas I let it out. One-half of a thimbleful at a time, so slowly that it hurt. And when my chest cavity was emptied, the still hollowness in the narrow thumbspace between my ribs seemed dangerous. Empty of oxygen and nitrogen and carbon dioxide, I had somehow contrarily expected to be lighter, for levitation to be a possible reality, but my feet didn't rise even two millimeters from the quiet earth.

Then I breathed in. That was all I did. I breathed out. Then in. And out again. The deliberate rhythm erased everything— the shrieks that were iron mallets against my skullbone, the surprising clean red of my sister's blood.

The day my mother shot my sister, I had skipped out

of school early because a blizzard was coming and I wanted some yarn. The weather was already pretty bad. Pretty bad, depending on how you feel about snow and cold. I didn't mind because I was sick of school—my classes were so ignorant and inconsequential—and I wanted eight thousand feet of snow to fall so that I could hole up in my room and knit until I could go out and lay in the sun come spring.

The snow was already deep enough that it caked on the legs of my jeans and dropped in damp icy lumps into my shoes. It was hard to hurry—there was that awful sensation of work that walking in snow or sand occasions—and I was hurrying because I was trying to sneak away before anyone saw me. I'd go to the Ben Franklin store for some yarn and then to the grocery store where I planned to splurge on the biggest bag of ruffled potato chips that I could find and a pint of cheap and fatty French onion dip.

I hated winter then and mostly I still do. At least I wasn't in that crappy, dilapidated shack that I'd always called home. If I was ever unfortunate enough to have kids, I'd never subject them to a domicile like that—a two-story hundred-year-old artifact with no insulation or central heat, no running water . . . Mom and Dad were obviously too stupid to bring up kids, and they must have hated us to boot. God, I was glad to be out of that dump. I was always cold. Dad would bellow, "If yer cold, put on some more damn clothes!" when I already felt so padded I could barely move, and it didn't do one thing to warm up the air I was taking in through my nose. All those layers of second-hand clothes made me feel too fat to be seen in public.

It didn't take me long to reach the Ben Franklin. Hardly anyone was there, which suited me fine. I hid two skeins of purple yarn inside my coat and bought two of white that were on sale. I was gonna knit an afghan with stripes. All I could do was the knit stitch—I couldn't even purl—but I wanted to knit and knit and zone out on the hypnotic movement of my hands. Then I went to the grocery store, got what I wanted, and slugged my way back to the dorm.

My roommate, whose life I had endeavored to make miserable, had moved out weeks ago, and I had the dreadful cubicle to myself. Dreadful, I remember, thinking of the split-pea-soup industrial green concrete block walls, plastered over with posters, but it was the Taj Mahal compared to my room at home, where a bottle of pop had once frozen overnight and where snow whistled in through the cracks around the windows.

I had two of everything: two chairs, two desks, two closets, two hard little beds. One radiator, which I sat on as soon as I locked the door behind me. I was still cold—the radiator wasn't all that hot. The building was old, and everything fun was a fire hazard—TV, refrigerator, hot plate. We all had record players, and I constantly played mine to drown out the racket of the garbage other people listened to. "You Light Up My Life" and "Just the Way You Are" still make me gag. I listened to Queen: "I've paid my dues / Time after time / I've done my sentence / But committed no crime." Indeed. A black rotary phone hung on the wall. I answered every third time it rang. Don't ask me why. It was symptomatic of my being a teenager.

I was pleased that I had the dorm mostly to myself. By 5 p.m., about the time darkness fell, campus was deserted. By 7:30 p.m., the streetlights revealed only drifts of white—no sidewalk, no boulevard cutting through campus. By 9 p.m., I had discovered that I was the only one on my floor, the silence inside as deep and as engulfing as the silence outside.

My knitting didn't last long. I was bored out of my mind after about twenty minutes, so I ate chips and dip in the bed I didn't sleep in while reading *Fear of Flying*. Risqué stuff in those days.

When the phone rang, I screamed and threw potato chips all over the room. I went to the bathroom so I wouldn't have to listen to it ring.

It rang several times Saturday morning. I was climbing the walls—time was hanging like something foul and stiff. I knitted some. I went to the library and looked through magazines. I checked all the pay phones and pop machines in the vicinity and netted $3.65. I decided I'd study some when I got back, but I soon lost interest in it. When the phone rang around one, I took off my shoe and slapped the phone with it until it quit ringing. Then I took a nap.

I woke up when a volley of snowballs began to rattle my

window. It was darkish outside, pouring snow. I was infuriated. I crashed the window open and yelled some non-gender-specific obscenity thick with gutturals.

"Shuddup or I'll knock the top of your head clean off!" was the response.

"What are you doing here?" I screamed. "Get away from me!"

"Don't you never answer your phone? We was calling all day."

"Go home!" I shrieked.

"You're coming with me."

I inserted some voluble profanity into the situation, but Dennis interrupted.

"Mom's done shot Darlene!" he yelled.

"Again?" I said.

—IX—

BACK TO THE PRESENT

"Why in the hell would I want to see Darlene?" I spit. "Finest piece of horse's ass that ever waddled its way out of Kentucky."

"Your heart is as black as a demon's," my saintly brother observes. "How long has it been since you've seen her?"

"How long? Longer than it's been since I set eyes on your sweet mug, bubby. Not long enough."

"You always did hate her."

"Damn straight. Gonna keep right on hating her, too. Look at what she did to Mom—"

"Look at what Mom did to her!" Dennis argues. "She shot her own daughter. Twice."

I shrug, wishing I'd insisted on driving—Dennis was still at the wheel. "It was just a BB gun."

"Daddy hit you with a belt once, and I bet you still ain't over that. The way you carried on—"

"I didn't do anything! I changed the channel on the TV! Big deal. He was in a crappy mood and he took it out on me. He never did have any sense. I had bruises on the backs of my legs for two weeks."

"Any scars?" he asks quietly. "Darlene's got big scars that look like half-rotted mushrooms—"

"Darlene's got scars, so she wins? Stop the car! Right now!"

"Sounds like somebody didn't get enough beauty sleep."

"I want to go home." I pout, knowing I'm pouting and not caring. "I hate this place. Get out. I want to drive."

"I think you just hate yourself."

"So you turned into a psychiatrist and a philosopher, too, and not just a criminal? Bet Mom's sure proud of you."

"There's a place to get coffee up ahead. You want some, or you just want to sit there and quarrel?"

"I want some coffee. Didn't you hear me say that something like a dozen times?"

"Pipe down, Poo. We're here."

He pulls my car into a gravel parking lot. There's a trailer spackled over with pink stucco, and around the window is hot pink neon tubing that spells out EATS. I swear to God. EATS. I am desperate enough that I go in of my own free will.

"Ought to be called DRINKS," I mumble to Dennis, and he almost smiles.

Inside, the place is warm and smells like cinnamon. It melts me, somehow, like butter. I'm a puddle of goo, and I like it.

"Let's sit," I say, and Dennis shrugs. Four people are already seated, and they stare at us like we're walking cabbages or something. Cowboys, every one of them, from boots to hats to the shirts with pearl snaps stretched tight over watermelon bellies.

Dennis nods at them, and we sit in the corner. The small round table is covered with silhouettes of moose and bear in profile in blue on a bright yellow background. The napkins are bandanas, kinda cute, but sort of disgusting as they make me think of snot.

"Black coffee," I say to the waitress, a thin Indian woman in worn blue jeans and a Bart Simpson sweatshirt that proclaims, *Eat my shorts!* Her hair and complexion are to die for. She looks tired but she smiles at us.

"And you, sir?"

"I want a piece of whatever it is you've been baking with all that cinnamon."

"I don't bake nothing," she says. "But I can bring you some. You want coffee, too?"

"Milk," he says, and I roll my eyes. Something about the idea of a huge overgrown human drinking baby food for calves is ridiculous.

She vanishes, and soon returns with our drinks and a chunk of steaming carrot cake about the size of a brick. The sound you hear is my jaw hitting the table.

"Godamighty," Dennis breathes. "Thank you, Honey."

"Don't flirt with the waitress," I say, inhaling the sweet aroma of my rich black coffee. "It's so common."

"Put a cork in it, Poo. Want some?"

"I thought you'd never ask."

He eyeballs me. "You buying?"

I whap him on the shoulder, and one of the cowboys laughs. I wink at him despite his gnarly ugliness, and Dennis says, "Don't flirt with the cowboys. It's so common."

Although my first impulse is to swear bawdily, I check it and plaster on an artificial grin instead. I sometimes worry about swearing too much, and it seems like I've been swearing a lot lately. It's like some part of me believes that all the words we utter stay out there, tangible, like invisible satellites monitoring us, and the words are pointy little pitchforks that come back to punish us when we least expect it. They don't poke us in the butt, that's too painless, but instead thread their way into our ear canals where they materialize into steel fishhooks.

I scare myself sometimes.

Like now. This present is pretty scary. I'm in a dive called EATS with a brother I haven't seen in thirteen years. My mother's stashed in another state doubtlessly running up a ferocious phone bill while she makes herself at home on the Internet. I am so disoriented that I don't know where I am and don't really care. And now this Dennis thing out of the blue wants me to visit a sister that I haven't seen since I was eighteen and who, quite frankly, I had gleefully convinced myself was dead.

At least the coffee is good. The cinnamon is so strong that I can still smell it. It makes me homesick for a home I've never had. We sit in silence until I drink up three cups' full.

"I have to think about it," I say finally. "I can't just walk in and say *Hello, good to see you.*"

"I guess," he says slowly. "I had to think long and hard before I decided it was all right to see you and Mom."

I nod. "Have you always been in touch with her?"

Then he nods. "Every single minute."

We are quiet for a little while. One of the cowboys winks at me when he leaves. I just stare at him. "You two always did like each other. I could never figure out why."

He sighs. "Me, neither. And I've spent a lot of time thinking about it. We ain't nothing alike. Never was. It's just one of them things."

"She knows we're here." If they're that close, he's told her.

"Of course."

"Does she want to see us?"

"She wants to see you. She's not sure about Mom. And I might as well tell you so you'll be over it before we get there. She's a college professor and in the second year of a MacArthur Fellowship."

"What's that?"

"It's sometimes called a genius grant. More money than you and me put together will ever make, spread out over three-year payments. She don't have to worry about working, but can just go around being a genius."

"And what is our sister a genius at?" I spit icily, becoming aware that I need desperately to go to the ladies' room.

"She's a volcanologist."

"What the hell's that?"

"She studies volcanoes. She's a professor somewhere in Hawaii, but she's here for the three years of her fellowship to study the volcanology of Yellowstone."

"Ain't no damn volcanoes in Yellowstone," I scoff. "Just a bunch of stinky geyser pools."

"Maybe you should apply for one of them MacArthur things. You're brilliant, too."

A good time to stalk off silently, with disdain. So I do. The bathroom is clean and warm, a big improvement over that moose pit stop in Cooke City.

Dennis is still sitting there at our table when I come back, so I pay our bill and head back to the car. My brother follows. I climb into the driver's seat of my very own abused blue car. Dennis hasn't returned the keys to me, but I fool him. I have a second set in the glove box. I pull them out and jingle them under his nose, then I stick my tongue out at him for good measure. He gets in the passenger side and slams the door. It doesn't mean he's angry, I've learned—just that he's a guy, and guys like to slap things around.

"So," he says. "Where we goin'? It's up to you."

"Maybe *we* ain't going anywhere." I haven't started the ignition yet. "I need some time to myself. *You* need to go see Mom. Don't see much of a we there."

"So where are you going?"

I shrug. "But you're going back to Kivic's Motel so you can pick up your truck and go down to visit Mom. She's old, Dennis, and this might be the last chance you ever have to see her—"

"I saw her a few days ago. And I might be seeing her this very minute if you wasn't such a bonehead. I sure wouldn't have to waste nonrenewable resources driving all the day down to Wyoming."

"We are *in* Wyoming," I declare, although we are not, having started the car and heading back in the direction from which we have just come.

"So where are you gonna take yourself?" he says after he belches very loudly.

California, I think, but mumble something about Kalispell. It's the only place I can think of in Montana.

"Kalispell," he scoffs. "You don't know where the hell Kalispell is. It's a day and a half's drive from here."

"Where's Darlene live?" I ask suddenly.

"None of your ever lovin' business," he retorts.

Good good good *god*, I think. It sure would be nice if I lived in a family that had at least one person in it that I liked. I might have liked one of my grandparents, but I could barely remember them. All of Mom's sisters were fruitcakes, and I hadn't seen any of my cousins since we were grown. I was finding that I could barely tolerate Dennis after an absence of more than a decade. I didn't really like Mom, but I was used to her. The tears that I had cried at my father's funeral had been tears of profound joy. As for Darlene . . . excuse me while I spit. I could spit bones thinking about her. Surprised by my long-simmering hatred? Don't be. The Simpkinses know all about grudges and feuds and all that hillbilliness.

It doesn't take me long to get back to Kivic's Motel, because, after all, we haven't gone very far. I park on the steep hill, pull up the emergency brake, and grin at my brother.

"Out, bubby," I say, gesturing with my head.

"Where are you going?" he repeats.

"Kalispell," I say, for the complete lack of anything else to say.

"Well, if you're dead-set on going there . . . ." He shrugs. "Let me at least give you a sack lunch for the road. How about it?"

"With a piece of that red velvet cake?"

"Sure."

We go back inside. "I'm going to the bathroom first. I'll see you in the kitchen," I say, and he nods.

But when I go to the kitchen, no one is there. "Dennis?" I call. "Jimmy?"

"Mrrink!" the cat says, and I look up to see Othello jump from one of the cabinets to the table. He poses, tail flicking, as though I should applaud.

I don't like the feeling that's suddenly rolling over in the depths of my bowels.

"Dennis!" I scream, and run for the door.

But I am too late. My car is gone and the dust has already settled.

—X—

IF SIMPLICITY IN LIFE IS THE KEY TO EVERYTHING . . .

and if solitude is the key to simplicity, then suddenly I find myself in heaven on earth.

My anger is gone in a flash, and I feel nothing but a sense of pure and sweet relief. At last, I am alone.

How long has it been since I've been alone? How many days and nights? Last night was the first time I'd slept in a room by myself since I'd started on this chaotic journey, and I was too worried about spies and impostors to be able to relax and savor it. Mom and I had been cooped up in the car together surely more than the chronological four days that the date on my watch showed me.

The sigh that escapes me is one of pure bliss.

I wander back into Kivic's Motel and wend my way back to the kitchen. I open the refrigerator door and find a note propped against a carton of soy milk. What kind of a dope drinks soy milk? Disgusting.

"Den," I read. Of course I roll my eyes. "My little brother tested positive for AIDS and tried to kill himself by driving into a floodwall. I've gone to be with the family—in Ohio. Don't know when I'll be back. I'll write or e-mail when I know something, but it'll probably be a couple of weeks before I get back. Sorry for the inconvenience. Jimmy."

Doesn't life change in the blink of an eyelash? An hour ago Jimmy was here, happy with his pancakes; now he was speeding east to attend a family disaster. I hope his family wasn't always a disaster, like mine was, is, and always will be.

I flop down at the yellow kitchen table. Othello presents

himself, and this time I am happy to oblige him. I like cats, though I've never been had by one. I pet him as long as he's agreeable, not really thinking about anything, my breathing calming to a slower rate than normal.

Perhaps I'll go back upstairs and take a nap . . . .

Then I wonder about the buffalo skull truck. I pick up the cat and hang him over my shoulder and go back to the front door. The truck's there in the parking lot. I leave Othello inside, making sure the door is unlocked, and saunter over to have a look. I open the door, but the keys aren't there. I hadn't really thought they would be. Plus, I remember that Jimmy had taken the battery out so nobody could mess with it. Even if I lucked into a key, there's no way I could put a battery in that truck and actually get it to work.

Suddenly the wind whips me. I wrap my arms around myself and shiver. I look at the sky. It's as heavy and gray as a bad dream. It can't be going to snow?

I hurry back inside, and I'm careful to latch the door behind me. I hurry through the living room—those feathered lampshades have got to go before I roll my eyes back so far in my head that they catch there—down the hall and back into the kitchen, where I make sure the back door, too, is secure. I grab a piece of cold fried chicken out of the fridge and dash back upstairs to the room where I'd spent the night, to e-mail Mom that Dennis is coming to see her, driving my car, and if he isn't there by dark to call the police and report my car as stolen. I give her the pertinent information: make, model, tag number. She hasn't sent me another message, but why should she? I shut everything down and proceed to wonder what to do next.

The obvious thing to do is snoop. Explore, if you will, every nook and cranny of this Kivic's Motel. In a way, I'd like to know what all is here, how many rooms are in this crazy place, and what's in each of them. For I am sure there are secrets here. I wouldn't be surprised to find a dungeon full of skeletons or a dragon guarding a treasure or a torture chamber or a den of rattlesnakes—or a greenhouse or an underground swimming pool or a gift-wrap design studio or a collection depot for the nearest Cougar Dive.

But in another way, I don't want to know. Because the more

I know, the more involved I'll likely become, and the more I'll care. I've spent my life not caring and I don't intend to start now. All I want to do in the whole wide world is go home.

God, I wish I was an orphan—raised in some filthy, poverty-struck orphanage by distantly kind but slovenly, apathetic pseudo-nuns; in other words, apathetic enough not to beat me since I'm not into pain. I'd have worn some kind of dowdy uniform with a pinafore and heavy black socks. More *Cider House Rules* than *Oliver Twist*. Then once I got out of their clutches I would have no possible reason to ever go back, no possible compulsion to keep in touch.

Instead I'm compulsed to keep in touch with my own blood kin, whom I don't even like. I mean, I guess I sort of like Mom, especially now that she's old enough not be dangerous any more. In the real world—and whoever would have thought that I, Cerise Cloudmist, would ever think of Kentucky as the real world—we live a couple of hours' drive apart. She lives in a little apartment building next door to some other old women, and they terrorize the neighborhood by looting yard sales, playing Rook, and bossing around the staff of the Senior Citizens Center. General Dunn Simpkins has been dead since I was twenty-six, and until just recently Dennis and Darlene have been invisible.

Darlene. Little Miss Priss Darlene. What a waste of the planet's natural resources, what a waste of all the food she's ever eaten, every piece of paper she ever read or wrote on. Talk about a pinafore. And Mary Janes and sweet blue ribbons in her hair, that was her. Like Dorothy in *The Wizard of Oz*, with that little hand pulled up and back all the time . . . . That she made a professor isn't anything unexpected. Prissy little damn bookworm. But a genius? Excuse me while I gag until I rupture eight percent of my internal organs. A genius?

No doubt Dennis had told her what I do for a living and they've had a good laugh over it. And while I'm thinking about it, I wonder what the hell Bristlehead does to earn his daily bread. Don't know that I believe that business about being a nightwatchman—sounds like a good excuse to go out at night and get into trouble. Surely he doesn't earn his keep blowing up snowmobiles. Maybe he's a petty thief on the side.

I go back up the stairs to the room. To *my* room. I might as well keep it. After all, I know that the armoire isn't a secret passageway and that the window is a fake. Lampshades made out of old brown turkey feathers and a fake window. Maybe Jimmy's grandfather, or whoever this Kivic was, was insane, with tacky taste and an oddball sense of humor.

I go over to look at the fake window. I guess it is a little more obvious in daylight, but not by much because there's just a little natural light coming into the room from the corridor. Yet it's not so hard now to see that there's no frame around the window, and there's no sill. Just a short pair of yellow gingham curtains stapled to the wall. Though I pull the panels back and feel the wall very carefully, I don't notice anything except a peely place in the wallpaper. I peel it some more, but underneath is merely another pattern of wallpaper.

I sigh, let the curtains fall, and turn around. Othello is sprawled across the pillows. I grin and go over to squeeze him up in my arms; he keeps his eyes closed and purrs louder. What a dollbaby. I seem to have made a friend. And I think I will nap for a minute . . . . When I get up, I'll look for a flashlight. And while I was outside, I should have looked—

I am upstairs in the old bedroom at Mamaw and Papaw Adkins' and it is the middle of the night, and I am squatting over the top of the pee bucket trying to keep its cold, thin metal rim from touching the skin of my backside. The moon is so bright I can clearly see everything inside the room—the enormous bed, the heavy furniture, I can see the moldy smell of the yellowing wallpaper, and I can see the gray boogery snores coming up out of Darlene's nose. I am lucid enough to wonder if I am dreaming, and when I reach for the pee bucket under me, I can't feel anything, so I stand up to find that I am sitting in a window seat on an airplane. I am sitting next to Peter Gabriel. I stare at him until I realize I don't care, then I resume looking out the window. Suddenly we hit a lot of turbulence and the plane starts dipping and jolting. I am not afraid and Peter isn't either because he continues to read as though he isn't anywhere at all. But a grayish-haired dumpy old woman rushes up to Peter with her purse hanging over her arm. "Oh, Peter," she wails, "can I worship you?"

Peter sighs in exasperation, as though he gets asked this all the time, and sticks his leg out into the aisle. The old woman falls to her knees and stretches out, the blue flowered fabric of her dress biting hard into her upper arms. Her knees primly together and her back straight, she presses her face into the floor and stretches her arms above her head until her hands reach Peter's feet. Then she pushes his pants leg up and pushes his sock down, and she clasps her hands together around his naked ankle, glued into this devoutly humble position. Peter continues to read. The woman begins to jabber, face-down in the aisle, and I cannot see any benign results of her worship. The plane lurches again.

Then I am in a hurricane and I am trying to run but I cannot get anywhere. My feet are locked in steel. I can't even inhale to scream. And someone like Fred Flintstone is coming up behind me with a club, except he's scary. I can see him coming and I know he's going to hurt me.

Then I realize I'm not dreaming but lying here in this bed in Montana and some ogre with a club is standing over me, and I still can't move. It's like my limbs are paralyzed. I feel tight in my stomach—

"*Waugh!*" I scream, flinging myself up. Othello looks at me like I am an idiot and yawns hugely like a pink staple remover. Of course no one is here. Stupid dream—I feel like I have been force-fed Silly Putty.

Ice. I won't vomit if I can suck on a piece of ice. I go back to the kitchen, where I can see that it is pouring snow. I run outside and look in the glove box in the truck, which is what I was thinking that I should have done earlier. It is empty. I look under the seats. Nothing but a scraper and a pair of men's drawers that have obviously been used as a clean-up rag after an oil check.

Already about two inches of snow have fallen.

Well, there's nothing for it but to lock myself in again and eat hugely. I have fun looting the larder. I eat a lot—cornbread, pickles, cold lasagna, another piece of fried chicken—then go to check my e-mail. There is no message from Mom, and I reluctantly decide I should call her—I have the receipt from the motel where I checked her in.

But of course I can't find a telephone. There is no telephone in this four-star exclusive motel. No phone.

No phone, no lights, no motor car, not a single luxury. So I push furniture against the doors, find a book (a Hardy Boys mystery, but I'm desperate), climb into bed with a box of glazed donuts, and read until sleep comes.

—XI—

SITUATION VACANT

The morning is peaceful, a deep silent snow erasing almost everything except tree and mountain. It is quite beautiful, I decide, though the thermometer reads fourteen degrees Fahrenheit. I am not sure what Othello should be fed for breakfast, though he's very vocal about insisting on its imminent appearance. He eats some zapped fried chicken (bone removed), smacking greasily while I wait for the coffee to make. I am glad the cat is here. Otherwise I might be a little claustrophobic in my solitude, but I figure no one can get in and, as far as I'm concerned, no one will even know I'm here. I look through the cabinets for something breakfasty. Lots of canned beef stew and tamales and Spam and stuff like that. Ah! Peanut butter and graham crackers. A fine breakfast for a stowaway princess. I eat over the sink so I can just wash the crumbs away.

The coffee is ready, so I pour myself a sizable serving (after warming my mug in the microwave—it's drafty in here and I hate cold coffee) and wander into the living room.

It's time to snoop.

And buddy, don't I. I find all kinds of tools, dirty things, junky stuff like rusted bed springs coils, empty boxes, probably a thousand pencils that have never been sharpened, envelopes postmarked from the forties with no letters inside, a desk with every drawer filled with staples, a carton of clipboards, hundreds of nails and screws, used matches, a stack of newspapers from Winchester, Illinois, and other sundries that make my hands dirty without being the least bit interesting.

The downstairs is all accessible: the big living room,

kitchen, laundry room, small bathroom, and two small rooms that I assume are Dennis' and Jimmy's because they look lived in. I don't investigate them too closely. Upstairs is the long corridor of motel rooms, with a bath at either end. There are a dozen guest rooms; mine is Number Four. Number Three looks much like mine, and I assume it would have been Mom's room. A lot of heavy furniture is in Number Six, Number Twelve is completely empty, and all the other doors are nailed shut. I can't budge them. I think of the flashlight which I hoped to find but did not, because I would have used it to try to look through the keyholes.

It suddenly hits me that since the Internet is in my room, there must also be a phone jack there. There is, and under the bed I find a wall phone. I plug it in, and—yes!—there's a dial tone.

I call Mom. She answers on the third ring.

"Who are you and what do you want?" a voice says, leaving me no doubt that I've reached the appropriate person.

"It's me, Mom. Are you okay?"

"Where are you?"

"I'm at Dennis's place—"

"What foolishness. I don't know how all that ignorance gets in your head. Brenda Marlene, of course that man's Dennis. I wouldn't have believed you if I hadn't been so tired and discombobulated."

"Is he there?"

"No." I make some wordless barking exclamation. "He's in his own room," she continues. "Why didn't you come back with him? We had the nicest time last night. We went to the gate made of elk antlers and ate cowboy pizza."

"I didn't come because he drove off and left me—"

"Well, you must have done something bad to him. He's as sweet as pie. He really is my son Dennis."

I sigh. "I know that, Mom. He's just different."

"He ain't the only one that's different," she says, managing to insinuate that I'm a nut case. "Why—"

I shamelessly interrupt. "What are y'all doing today?"

"I don't necessarily know that I've decided."

"Did it snow there?"

"Where?"

"Don't start that with me! Are you snowed in there?"

"Brenda Marlene, all the time and money I spent on you for you to turn out like this. I might as well have give you up to be adopted for all the good you've done me."

"You got twenty seconds to talk sense or I hang up."

"Who died and made you king? You're the one that called here, remember?"

"Fifteen. Fourteen."

She is silent.

". . Five. Four. . ."

"Nope."

"Nope what?"

"Nope, it didn't snow. It's September. It doesn't snow in September. Are you at Yellowstone? What time is it up there?"

"Same time as it is where you are."

"Well, what time is it at home? I think maybe my biological clock is still on Kentucky time. My bowels—"

I don't want to hear about Mom's bowels. "Why don't y'all come and get me?"

"Why didn't you come with Dennis?"

"Because he drove off and left me!" I scream. "On purpose! I'm snowed in and Jimmy's gone and Dennis has stole my car. If he's not back here by," I look at my watch, "three this afternoon I'm telling the police that he stole my car."

"That would be stupid. They'd just impound it for evidence and then we'd have to fly home."

Not a bad idea . . . I am shocked in a thoroughly marvelous way.

"Are you there, Brenda? Are you behaving yourself?"

I find my tongue. "Where has that ever got me?" Fly home?

"Honey, you ain't never tried it. I had the weirdest dream last night—"

"Where's Dennis?"

"I done already told you. He's in his room."

"Asleep at a quarter to ten? I don't think so. Look out in the parking lot and see if you see my car."

"You are the aggravatingest child that ever lived." But I

hear her put down the phone, then I hear footsteps, a pause, more footsteps, and then she picks up the phone. "It's there, filthy as shit. Are you happy now? I guess you think we're going to wash it for you, but you can just think again."

"I guess you got up on the wrong side of the bed and walked plumb into the wall and then your breakfast was greasy."

"It wasn't greasy enough. Are you ready to go home yet?"

"I thought you were having such a great time with your son. Perhaps you should spend at least another week enjoying one another's company."

She is silent, and I'm not sure whether it's with disapproval or some kind of conniving that it takes all her energy to concentrate on. I wish she'd think more often and cut down on the level of noise pollution. I wish I knew what I'd said, so I can say it several times on the way home. If the trip out here was bad, the trip home will be a foreign language horror movie.

"So where you at?" she finally says.

"I'm at Dennis's place. Not that Cooke City place, but the Victorian bed and breakfast where he wanted us to go? It's just an old hotel."

"Well, do tell. Our Dennis owns a hotel?"

"He doesn't own it," I say quickly, before she lets herself get too impressed. "He just lives there. And it's not a hotel, not a real hotel. They don't have guests or anything. It's just your basic uninhabitable wreck, exactly the kind of place you'd expect Dennis to live in. A pure mess," I say gleefully.

"At least it ain't a trailer," my sainted mother retorts.

"Let's not start. Please pass my message on to my brother. If he's not here by three, I'm reporting him. You might remind him that he told me something last night that I can blackmail him with. You might also remind him that I'm not above doing exactly that. Three p.m. right here, today. Got that?"

I can see her pout all the way from Jackson. "You're always so mean to me," she snivels. "Dennis is so nice."

"He wouldn't be if he knew you as well as I do. He'd be a regular butthole, too." I don't give her time to say anything. "Now what are you going to tell Dennis when you finally see him this morning?"

"I'm gonna tell him that you're as full of shit as a Christmas turkey." She hangs up.

Well, she not going to beat me. I call the front desk and check her out. Take that, Mommie dearest. Then I slam down the phone, and with a sigh I wander over to peer out the window. But of course it isn't a window.

Welcome to Kivic's Motel. You can't check in and you can't check out . . . .

A horn blows outside. I hurry downstairs and peek out the front. The sun is out and most of the snow has melted to slush. There is a car in the parking lot.

I open the front door and stick my head out.

"Hey!" some guy yells. "You got any rooms?"

I shrug. "Sure," I say. "Come on in."

—XII—

GUESTS THAT PAY, IN MORE WAYS THAN ONE

. . . heh heh heh . . .

Don't ask me why I said that: I don't know and I don't care. If the Army had come by wanting to sit in a Hummer in the parking lot and lob hand grenades through the window, I would have politely acquiesced. It was a way to poke my fingers in Dennis' eyes, figuratively speaking.

And just as immediately I want to take back the words I'd said, especially when I see four people get out of the car. I will let them come in, I am thinking wildly, and then I will leave.

But I don't know how.

The people are so bundled up that I can't tell whether they're male or female. They hurry inside, without having lugged out a bunch of stuff. I hold the door open and they pass through.

"This isn't really a motel," I say.

"I don't care. It's warm. That's all I care about. Warmth," comes from a definitely female voice. "God, I'm so cold."

"The heater doesn't work in the car," comes another voice, a male voice that certainly has an MBA behind it.

"Then Frank screwed up the window, taking a picture of a bear," this voice was mocking, "and now we're driving around in this blizzard with the window down. Jesus, my nose. I'll probably lose it."

"Then you can stop sticking it in everyone else's business. You bunch of weenies. I'm Frank," Frank says to me, extending a hand inside an oversized glove big enough to belong to an astronaut, "Frank Button."

"Hello, Frank Button," I say, shaking his paw. "I'm Ce— Brenda. Brenda, uh, Sims. Welcome to Kivic's Motel."

"You got a woodstove or any place I can warm my hands?" asks the only definitely female voice.

"No, but I'll make you something hot to drink. Please have a seat—"

"Can I come to the kitchen and turn on a burner and hold my hands over it? Please?" she asks.

I shrug. "Sure." They all follow me to the kitchen.

I put on water to boil. The woman turns the oven on at four hundred degrees and opens the door. They gather around it, bouncing up and down. I start another pot of coffee.

"Where y'all from?" I ask, somehow desperate to make conversation and make these people happy.

"Ohio. West Union," says Frank. "We're a long way from home."

"Me, too," I say. "I'm from Carter County, Kentucky."

"What are you doing here?" the woman asks. She's taken off her gloves and her fingers are a scary-looking lilac. "My name's Christy. He's my brother."

Frank grins.

"This is my brother's place. He's out running errands," I say. "He and some other guy caretake it for the owner. It's some kind of weird," I say, deciding to state the obvious.

"It's warm," says MBA voice, "so that makes it some kind of marvelous."

I am going through cabinets looking for tea and cocoa, but the only thing I find that I can make with hot water is instant grits with fake ham flavoring. It sounds revolting.

"Are you hungry?" I ask stupidly. Of course they are, so I make them each a cup of grits, and once I get them away from the stove I scramble a dozen eggs and warm up the cornbread in the microwave. By this time the coffee is ready, and they eat and eat, and I find that I've stopped listening to what they're talking about. I don't check back in until MBA voice asks what they owe me.

I shake my head. "You don't owe me anything. I told you, this isn't really a motel. I'm glad to have some company," I say, surprised to find it's true.

"At least let me help you clean up," MBA says. "I owe you something."

So the others adjourn to the living room with coffee, warm enough to shed coats and assume human form, and he and I clean up. The kitchen is a terrible mess, but he's too polite to say anything about it.

His name is Boone Clinton, and he and Frank and Christy Button and the other person, Loretta Catron, are all cousins who grew up together and who hadn't been in contact since they were children. So they decided to get together and drive to Twin Bridges, Montana, to visit another cousin who has a sheep ranch there. They've been out here a little over a week and it hasn't been the family reunion of anyone's dreams. None of them got along with the sheepster cousin's wife, so they left sooner than they'd planned. Boone likes Frank, despite Frank's immaturity (he doesn't go into details at this point), but the girls drive him nuts, always having to blow-dry their hair and worrying about how they smell "in the wilderness!" he exclaims in disbelief. They are here because they got lost in the weather; they have been in Yellowstone. Boone is still elated from the magnificence of it, but Frank, he says, was always wanting to throw things into the geyser pools and off the overlooks—probably just a joke, but Boone worried. And then the girls and their mirrors . . . .

So I tell him most everything that has happened to me on this ignorant trip. To my surprise, I am able to transform much of the agony into comedy, especially the part about suspecting that Dennis is an impostor. I like hearing Boone's laughter. I like the way he washes dishes. I like the way he stands there on the floor. I like the way *he* is being polite to *me*, a Simpkins. I just plain like the way he takes up space.

I could have babbled forever, but of course we finish too soon. We each take a cup of coffee into the living room.

"Why am I not surprised?" Boone mutters when we see that Frank has one of the feathered lampshades on his head. "See?"

I laugh even though I am also appalled, because the dust and decades-old bird mites that could be in those feathers . . . well, I sure wouldn't want that on my head. I hope Frank doesn't have allergies or asthma or he just might choke to death here in good ole Kivic's Motel.

"So, is this place real or what?" Loretta asks. She is built like a linebacker, with carefully permed and pomaded champagne-colored hair and aubergine lipstick, both of which clash terribly with the color of her skin.

"Surely we are not collectively dreaming," I say. It comes out more snottily than I intend, but no one seems to have noticed because they are rubbernecking the contents of the room, which I've already processed. "So. Where are you going?" I ask brightly. I'm suddenly so very tired of them, except maybe Boone, and it's getting close to one o'clock. If Mom and Dennis left soon after I called, they could be here any minute.

"Home, I guess," Frank says. What a stupid name—Frank Button. It can't be real. "I've used up all my film."

"There are stores out here," I say, wondering why I'm defending this apathetic place. No, the place is not apathetic, I am apathetic about it.

"You got a phone here?" Loretta asks.

"No," I say. There's no phone for her. Unreasonably, I hate her. I wish she were the one sitting there with an infectious lamp shade on her head. I'd sneak up on her and crack her clavicles with a ballpeen hammer.

"Where's the nearest town?" Boone asks.

"Probably Gardiner. It's right next to Yellowstone. You probably went through it to come here."

"Would there be an auto repair place there?"

"My guess is that everything that a hapless tourist might need can be found there."

Frank laughs.

"Could you give me a lift into town?" Boone asks.

"I would if I could," I say. "But that truck out there? It doesn't run."

"How'd you get here?" Christy asks.

"My brother has my car. He's gone to pick up our mother. But we can probably find some plastic or cardboard to duct tape over that window—"

"I am not going anywhere until that heater is fixed," Christy declares.

"That's a hell of a thing to say," comes out of me before I have a chance to think about it. "You just roll in out of the blue and eat my food and act like you own the place. I done told you this ain't no motel. I don't care if you warm up a little bit, but you ain't staying. None of you."

"We'll pay you—" Christy begins.

"That's not the point. I am going to be in big trouble if you all are still here when my brother gets back. He's . . . he's unpredictable."

"Violent?" asks Loretta, looking ready to take him on.

I shrug. "I think he's under investigation by the FBI," I boldly lie. "He witnessed some kind of murder and he's hiding out here. They've told him he's in a witness protection plan, but really they have him here to keep an eye on him, because they think he had something to do with it, too. He's a murder suspect."

"So you just waltzed in for a visit?"

"My mother's dying. He's her only son. She wanted to see him one last time before she goes."

"And you had to bring him a car from Kentucky?" asks the lampshade.

"It's a long story. And it's none of your business," I say pointedly. "And he should be back any time. I know where the duct tape is—"

"I've got a phone, Loretta," says Christy. "In my pack. A cell phone."

Hooray for modern technology, I think.

"Then haul it out and call Triple A," she says. "I need civilization. I might get *unpredictable* if I don't get some soon." She glares at me.

"You live in Peebles, Ohio, for pete's sake," Frank says. "Let me assure you that that is not civilization. Gay Paree, perhaps, but not—"

"Shut up," she says. "Christy, where's the damn phone?"

Christy starts rummaging in the bag she brought in with her. "Knock knock," says Frank. Luckily everyone ignores him.

I glance at my watch, and when I look up I notice that Boone is staring at me. His eyebrows look like two big woolly worms ready to lick out his eyes. His irises look like blue Cheerios floating in the milk of his eyeballs. Now I don't like so much the way he's taking up space.

"Knock knock!" Frank calls louder.

Loretta has the tiny cell phone pressed to her ear, looking as ignorant and as possessed as all cell phone users do. She is impatiently waiting for an answer. Her legs are crossed, and the foot that is in the air is kicking crazily.

I stare back at Boone. "Thank God," I hear Loretta say.

"Quit looking at me," I mouth to Boone.

"You're beautiful," he mouths back. Where's the Sultan's Kiss when I need it?

"Where the hell *are* we?" Loretta yells.

"Kivic's Motel," says Frank.

"Where's that?" she squalls.

"North of the north entrance," I say to her. Then I say to Boone, "Then take a picture."

"I am," he whispers.

"North of what?" she screams.

"Yellowstone," Boone says, looking at me.

"Yellowstone!" Frank screams. "Knock knock!"

"Frank, shut up," Christy says quietly, almost as though she's praying.

Suddenly I like her more than any of the others. "I'm sorry that I yelled at you," I say. "It wasn't you."

She smiles. "I understand," she says, and I believe she does. Even my family doesn't act this ignorant in front of strangers. Maybe life isn't so bad after all.

"Come with us," Boone mouths.

I just shake my head.

"They're coming!" Loretta yells, handing the phone back to Christy. "They're coming! They actually know where this hellhole is!"

I pick up a snowglobe from the table and throw it at her. "Take this as a souvenir," I say, "and never come back."

"You want the food back that I ate?" Loretta hefts the snowglobe like it's a big rock and she's a bully.

I start to say something about her mother was probably sorry she went through the physical agony of childbirth to bring a boob like her into the world, then I realize that I behave worse around my mother than I do anyone else in the universe, and I keep my mouth shut. Instead I pick up a telephone book from the table; it's from Louisiana. "Take this, too," I say, and throw it at her.

"I want that," says Frank, grabbing it from her. She grabs it back and slaps him with it. "Can I have this lampshade, too?"

"It's an antique," I say, "an artifact of historic Montana."

"I'll give you five dollars for it," he says.

"It's not for sale."

"Fifteen."

"No," I say. "Get it off your head. Put it back on the lamp before you damage it. You look ridiculous."

"Thank you."

"Come with us," Boone repeats softly. "You don't belong here."

"I sure as hell don't belong with you," I retort. "Put a sock in it."

"I love sassy women," he purrs.

God, a Don Juan to go with the idiot and the bully and the doll. Don't they all deserve each other. All we need is a belly dancer and a fireman and a preacher man and a beautician. We could make a new town.

"I hear something outside!" I exclaim. I don't, but it gets them all to the window and thinking about something else.

"I don't see anything," says Loretta.

"Got your eyes open?" asks Frank.

"Button it, Frank," says Boone.

"Ha ha," says Frank.

I am thinking that I will go upstairs and lock myself in my room, or rush out the back door and flag down a truck driver and get myself away from here, anywhere but here. I don't want to see Mom; I don't want to see Dennis; I sure don't want to see Darlene. All I want to see is the inside of my tiny, second-hand trailer on the outskirts of Olive Hill, Kentucky, and lock the door and curl up on the couch and sleep until spring. I hate this place. I hate my family. I hate myself. Instead I look out the window with the others and watch a wrecker pull into the parking area. I think the cousins are more relieved than I am.

"Go with us," Boone whispers yet again.

"Do you have some kind of auditory disorder, like selective deafness?" I retort, but part of me wants to say: Ask me again. And when he does I'll say: Hold on until I run upstairs and get my bag; and then I'll let him drop me off at any place with an airport . . . but I want my car. Bristlehead can have Mom, but he ain't keeping my car. It's paid for. And in the line of work I'm in, that means something.

"This is the last time I'm asking," he whispers, like he's overacting in some underbudgeted movie.

"Then this is the last time I have to say *No*," I say loudly, tact not being one of my strong points. "I have unfinished business here."

The guys go out and help the Triple A man fool with the car. Finally the girls go out. They get in the wrecker cab with the mechanic, and Boone and Frank get in their own car, and they all leave.

I am alone again.

—XIII—

PARTIAL DENOUEMENT

They are not here by five p.m., so I call the police and report my car stolen. Two days later some cops come by to tell me that my car has been found in the Taggart Lake parking area at Grand Teton National Park, abandoned. The car was first seen the previous day around noon, and when it was still there this morning, a park ranger checked the license number for the heck of it and found it had been reported stolen. I tell them about Dennis and Mom, but no one has seen them. It's a slow day, they continue, and offer to take me down to get my car. I get my things and happily leave with them. They give me a donut and pour me a cup of coffee from a thermos. I consume both.

When we reach my car, they stay with me while I check it out and start it. There is plenty of gas, and the car is terribly clean on the inside. The insurance and registration papers are in the glove box. I thank the policemen and they leave.

I sit in the car with the window down, even though the air is a little chilly. The sun is shining, though, and there is no snow here. I wish for my jacket. Wouldn't it be great if my luggage were in the trunk? I'd really like to see my stuff again. I get out and open the trunk. It is empty except for one pristine tube of Harem Heartbeat.

I'm thinking about my things, *my bag* that I brought with me from Kivic's Motel. It's a backpack that I found in the laundry room, a medium-sized green one. When I left Mom to find Dennis, I didn't take anything with me. No extra clothes, no shampoo or anything. So while I was snooping, I helped myself to a few pairs of socks, a bright pink tee shirt that says *Citizens for a Poodle-Free Montana*, and a black buffalo-plaid flannel shirt with iron-on denim patches on the elbows. They almost fit me so they must've been Jimmy's, and I sort of feel bad about stealing his things, but I didn't want anything of Dennis's to touch my skin. I wish I had stolen a sweatshirt or a jacket. I reach inside the pack and pull out the flannel shirt and slip it on.

I'm sure this is a very lovely place, but I don't feel like hiking. Now what? I have a credit card, but not much actual cash left. At least I have my car and a full tank of gas. I sit quietly for a few minutes. Then I know. I start the car and head south.

—XIV—

GOODBYE: THAT'S ALL SHE WROTE

I drive slowly. Now that I've formulated a plan, I'm not in such a hurry. A kind of peace has come over me, and luckily I have enough sense not to clutch at it and choke it. It's pink and sparkling, soft. A herd of about fifty wapiti lingers between here and the horizon. I feel sure that Mom has taken a picture of them, and maybe bought a postcard. I hope she was wearing her lipstick.

Back in Jackson, I go to the motel where I'd left Mom. I have my story ready.

"Hi," I say to the vapid-eyed geezer behind the counter. "My name is Cerise Cloudmist. My mother and I spent two nights here earlier in the week, and we've misplaced a piece of luggage. I was wondering if we might have left it here?"

"What room?" he asks brusquely.

"I don't remember."

"Can you describe the luggage?"

"It's my mother's. I don't remember exactly, but I'll recognize it when I see it. It's red."

The geezer looks suspicious. "What was in it?"

"Clothes. Toiletries." I shrug.

"One moment." He disappears into an office off to the left, closes the door, opens it again, and beckons to me. I walk behind the counter and its attendant computer paraphernalia.

"This is where we keep Lost and Found." He gestures toward an open closet. "See anything familiar in there?"

I emit some kind of bubbly sound, too happy to say a word.

My dirty red duffel bag has been flung on top of the pile. "That one!" I say, and grab it.

I can't believe it! I just can't believe it! Something good has happened. Perhaps my luck has finally changed.

The geezer insists on opening it, so we do. Inside are my wrinkled-up Carter County clothes and my little plastic container of Burt's Bees sample products, mostly used up. Reluctantly he lets me have my own stuff—my butter-yellow shirt!—all the while insinuating that there must be guns, illegal drugs, or contraband jewelry cleverly hidden somewhere inside.

I run back to the car, hugging my bag. My car! My clothes! I put the bag on the passenger seat, keeping my right hand on it as I re-enter traffic. I remember where the McDonald's is, and I go there before I pilfer through my bag. I park as far from any entrance as I can, for the relative privacy. I want to see my things again, but, more importantly, I want to change clothes.

I choose a pair of pleated khakis, a long-sleeved white tee, clean socks and underwear, and a pine-green windbreaker with a hood. I wrap everything up inside the windbreaker and carry it into the bathroom. As I slip them on, I am aware that the clothes actually smell clean. I wish I'd brought in some lotion. I took a shower before I left Kivic's, and my skin feels grateful for the clean, albeit very wrinkled, garments I'm helping it into. My feet want to dance, my hands to clap, my voice to shout AMEN! My brain restrains them, though it lets me laugh out loud here in the largest stall. I suddenly feel vastly superior to all the people out in the eating room and idling at the drive-thru. I have gone through the fire, and they've done nothing but sit around and consume numbly since they've been born. I throw my bad mood away with my old cotton drawers.

I ponder leaving the cat-burglar clothes in the trash too, but I'm still a long way from home, so I fold them up and stick them under my arm. I go out to the counter and get a supersize Number Five, and take it out to eat in the car while I look at my map.

I am really getting sick of this part of the country. If I were at home, in a sensible place, I'd have at least three different ways to get anywhere. But here, I go either the only way there is, or I don't go. I eat greedily, wiping my fingers on the map. There is only one way to go, so I will go that way.

I'm ready to get this show on the road. I'm ready to close it out and go home. I want to sleep in my own bed, wake up to familiar sights and familiar smells, I want to go to my dorky little job and pretend I never heard of Wyoming or Montana, Dennis or Darlene.

I lick my fingers, take a big draw on my pop, and belch. There ain't nothing like a good gut-shaking burp. I look down at my "clean" clothes and grin. My belly is full. Life is definitely better. Now I just have to find Mom and we'll go home. I'll put her in the trunk bound and gagged and drive it straight through.

My plan, such as it is, is to go back to Dennis's shack at Cooke City, and, if they're not there, it'll be back to Kivic's Motel for this Blue Kentucky Girl.

I ball up my trash and carry it inside to properly dispose of, because I've decided to take advantage of this pit stop while I can before I head back north.

The day is beautiful, I realize. Everything I see looks like I should be on a calendar: snow on sunny mountain peaks, yellow aspens, blue sparkling water, green fields dotted with elk in some places, buffalo in others. The air is cool but it feels good, easily breathable. Nothing smells bad. The world is so quiet. That's new for me. My thoughts are quiet, too, despite being multi-syllabic; they sound like shiny pennies sliding into a pink ceramic piggy bank and clinking onto a mounded nest of welcoming even shinier pennies. Then they sound like my four tires spinning on asphalt, then they sound like my breath. And suddenly I can't understand what I've been so upset about.

I'm clean and I'm full and I'm quiet, and I don't think I'd even mind having some pie and coffee with my big sister Linda Darlene Simpkins.

Isn't that cute? Linda Darlene and Brenda Marlene. Excuse me while I spit. If I didn't know better, I'd swear that she was adopted, and what makes me know better is that she's got that same old hillbilly face the rest of us have, except early on she learned how to set her mouth different so she didn't look so much like she'd crawled out from under a tarpaper shack.

She was a terrible big sister. She always sat properly, this in the days when girls had to wear dresses to school so it actually mattered. Her knee socks always stayed up. She made A's on everything. She had legible handwriting. She liked jazz, with all those horns sounding like a flock of geese being strangled. She'd won a scholarship to the University of Kentucky by the time she was a sophomore in high school. She talked like she grew up with Walter Cronkite for a daddy. She was perfect. She was always right. She knew everything.

Except how to be human.

Mom and Dad weren't et up with brains or perception, but even they could see right through her. They weren't fooled by all that muck she spouted all the time. "Shape up—your sister's looking up to you," Daddy used to tell her, but she was always a self-centered snot. She just stuck that little nose into the air, holding a big stack of books and mincing around in her clean little shoes. She kept herself shut up in her prissy neat room, improving herself. Half the time we forgot she was there until she waltzed down the stairs at suppertime wondering why we had to have fried baloney and fried potatoes and mustard greens and cornbread again. I mean, it wasn't my favorite either, but I was always hungry and it was food, so I ate it.

"What would be suitable for you?" Mom asked her once.

"Quiche Lorraine," she replied promptly.

"Sounds like some disease," Daddy said. "A giraffe disease."

"It's just eggs," Dennis said, "eggs in a pie."

"If that don't beat all," Daddy said.

"You mean custard?" Mom asked. "You want custard?"

Darlene rolled her eyes and launched into some explanation using so many French words that Daddy announced that he'd blister her rear end if she didn't stop using such language.

But there's no point in bringing up yesterday's news, the meeting's old business. I'll file her away in the same drawer I'm putting Dennis back into once I get Mom away from him and we're on the other side of the Mississippi.

I keep the mouth of my mind mostly shut and manage to make the long drive (everything out here is so far apart!) in peace and restfulness.

COOKE CITY

It's still daylight when I reach Cooke City. It looks the same as it did a few days ago, though this time I'm not surprised by it. This is a foolish thing I'm doing. I know it, yet I have recently done so very many foolish things that they're getting so they don't bother me. I pass the Moose Lick Café—I will stop there for a Teddyburger on my way back to Kivic's Motel.

I do not see Dennis's truck parked anywhere along the main drag. Did I expect to? I don't know. Do I expect to see him at his hovel? No. Then why am I going? Because my gut, my intuition, tells me that I must. And I'm sort of afraid that I'll find Mom tied up and left to die in that shack.

There. I've gone and thought it out loud. I'm afraid Dennis will hurt Mom, physically hurt her. Why? I don't know that, either. But I don't trust him. Mom's pretty scrappy when she gets in a corner, but Dennis is way bigger and he's a guy. He's confessed to blowing up snowmobiles, and it's no telling what other violences he has committed and never said a word about. He might just be more related to his daddy than he lets on.

I don't miss the turn this time, and park where I did before. It feels good to be out of the car—I've driven from Jackson without a stop.

It's so quiet—I can't hear anything except the whistle of the evening's cool wind. I put on the butter-yellow shirt again—I'm thinking mighty strong thoughts about yellow and I'm thinking that perhaps Cerise isn't quite yellow enough—and I get my first inkling of understanding. Suddenly I sort of know why he lives out here, why he breaks the law just to protect the silence.

There's not even much noise when I squat behind a boulder and pee.

Now that I'm here, I don't want to walk the scrubby little trail that goes to the cabin. The light is wintry thin. I bet it's scary out here the eighth of January, still on the wrong side of helplessness that Spring will ever come again. You've come this far, Brenda Marlene Simpkins Starflower Jade-Eagle Cerise Cloudmist. Do it and get it over with.

I sneak. It's not the thought of bears and cougars and wolves the way it was before, but somewhere in the back of my mind is the image of scabbed-over blood.

I thrash my way through the underbrush. That makes it sound like a jungle, and it was as far as I was concerned. I stomp my way to the shack and look at it for a few minutes. It's as forlorn and helpless-looking as it was the last time. The door's gaped open a little, and I can't remember if it was this way before. It doesn't matter. I don't bleat out Dennis's name this time, but as carefully and as quietly as I can I make my way to the door and push it open enough that I can ease myself inside.

The windows are curtainless, so I can see well enough. What little furniture there is looks homemade and is lying on its side. It's one smallish room as far as I can tell, but there's something that doesn't look right. A box in the far corner, filthy as everything else but with a clean black strip of webbing, like from a backpack, snaking out of the near corner.

I don't kick the box first but yank it up clean and quick. Historic Montana dust rises in the air. A small hunched-over woman winces and looks up at me.

"Looking for a volcano?" I shout.

—XVI—

THE GENIUS

It's the genius, of course. I'd know her anywhere.

"Get up out of the floor," I say. "You look ridiculous."

"What are you doing here?" she says, lithely standing up and dusting herself off.

"I suppose you live under that box? Is that where you're doing your research about the volcanoes of Yellowstone?"

"How did you know about this place?"

"This is where Dennis told us he lived. *He* gave *me* directions."

We look at each other, not quite glaring but almost. She has changed some. Her face and neck are more lined than mine, but she's much slimmer. Her blonde hair (she's a natural blonde, of course, that recessive little runt) is cut very short, and she's wearing leggings and a heavy cable tunic sweater so that she looks like a pixie. She doesn't look anything like a genius scientist. There's no telling what she thinks of me, and I suddenly, desperately, want her to think I'm pretty. I'm not; I never was.

"I'm glad to see you, Brenda," she says softly, and smiles, dirt streaked across her face.

Something clutches up inside of me and breaks open. I find that I'm crying, sobbing, bawling, gulping, making terrible ripping sounds inside my throat. I can't see and I can't hardly breathe for all the gunk trying to come out my nose. She comes to hug me and I turn away, but she puts her arms around me from behind and lays her head on my shoulder. It feels like my whole life cracking open. It is both horrible and wonderful because I know that nothing will ever be the same again. My shell is lying on the floor of this filthy cabin, and I know I'll never be able to put it back together again so that it will hold and protect me.

The sky darkens—the sun has slipped behind something—and I croak, "I've got to blow my nose or I'm going to drown in my own snot." She gives me a final squeeze and I blindly fish in a pocket for a tissue. I clean myself up as best as I can, and I find that when I turn around to face her I'm grinning. I don't want to, but I can't help it. I'm grinning like a monkey. She's grinning like a monkey.

"We finally grew up, Brenda." I can see that she's been crying, too. "We did it. We finally grew up. We made it."

I nod and sniff. "I'm sorry," I say. "I'm sorry for every stupid thing that ever happened."

We both sigh and look away.

"Me, too," Darlene whispers. Then she says, "Are you hungry?"

"I'm always hungry," I say. "Let's go to the Moose Lick Café for a Teddyburger. I'll drive," I hasten to add, vowing on the spot, despite my newly squishy heart, to never again voluntarily be a passenger while one of my siblings is behind the wheel.

"Oh, we don't need to drive. It's just over there." She points over what looks to me like a brush thicket. I somehow believe her, but all these years of suspicion die hard.

"I don't want to walk back up here in the dark," I say. "Hop in."

She shakes her head. "I'll meet you there," and she takes off like a little bunny.

I fish in my pocket for a tissue and blow my nose. I really want to throw it down and leave it on the floor, but the tissue is so white and clean and perfectly anomalous amongst all this mountain man squalor that I just can't. I walk to my car slowly, glad for a few minutes with my private self before walking into whatever happens with Darlene.

She is waiting for me outside the door. I park along the street, lock the doors, and clomp my way up the plank sidewalk to meet her. And suddenly I don't want to do this. Now that we've made up, I don't know that I have anything to say to her. She's been invisible for far too long.

We go in. The place is oddly familiar, yet oddly remote. I

feel like I'm in a movie. A pretty boring movie. We are playing the scene of the estranged sisters breaking bread together after two decades. She and I are strangers, despite the familiarity of our shared genes. We both order Teddyburgers and sit there in silence.

"Why were you hiding under that box?" I ask suddenly. I feel caught off guard that I didn't remember this sooner. I'm slipping.

She's cool. "How did you know I was there?" she asks.

"The belt of your backpack was sticking out. It was way too clean for the rest of that place."

"Touché, Sherlock," she says. "What were you doing there?"

"I asked first."

We stare at each other for a few seconds, and I guess she can see that I'm not backing down on this. "Looking for signs of volcanic activity?" I make a face that I hope means I'm arching my eyebrow. I realize belatedly that I'm repeating myself. My brain sure is on disconnect.

She laughs. "Looking for signs of intelligent life."

"Under a box?"

"I was looking for Dennis," she says.

"Me, too," I say, proud I don't question whether Dennis is intelligent life. "Dennis and Mom."

She looks too alarmed, and my defenses go up. She has to be faking something, hiding something. But I tell her, briefly, what's happened in the past few days. Darlene looks concerned, and I know that if she says anything about *foul play* that I'll start laughing, and laugh until my stomach muscles cramp up. It's been a long time since I've done that, and I'm not particularly looking forward to doing it again.

She's quiet. It's her turn to say something, and she knows it. So I stare at her. To my surprise, she picks up her empty plate and licks every crumb off it. I continue staring, because she has just broken a bit of my mental image of her, and she knows that too. I feel much more wary. I didn't expect this kind of cunning from her.

"When was the last time you were in contact with Dennis?"

She shrugs. "It's been a few days."

I'm intuiting that she's wondering if I know about Dennis's monkeywrenching and whether I approve of it. I'm wondering if she's aiding and abetting him. I sure hope so, because I'd love to have some blackmail material on her, too.

"He told me about the snowmobiles," I offer.

She waves her hand dismissively. "This doesn't have anything to do with that."

I'm tired of this, tired of her. "Look," I say, "I just want to go home. Once I find Mom, I'm outta here. Where would Dennis take her?"

"Not to my place?" Darlene looks suddenly terrified.

"No. I think he'd try to protect you from her."

"I need it," she says quietly, looking away. "She shot me."

"Yeah, I know." It's my turn to wave my hand dismissively. "Twice. Holy shit, Darlene, she shot you with a BB gun, not an AK47, about five million years ago. Get over it."

"That's easy for you to say." How predictable. That silly woman.

"You have scars," I say. She looks up at me quickly, alarmed. "Dennis told me. You know what I told him? I told him that we all have scars. Everybody has scars. Yours are on the outside. The rest of us have scars on the inside." You know, of course, that I never told Dennis any such thing.

"You think I don't have scars on the inside?"

"I never said that. I'm just saying that you're not the only one. You are not unique. You are not the only one with permanent damage inflicted by this dysfunctional family. You inflicted some of my scars. I inflicted some of yours. Dad was an asshole. I hated him. I'm glad he's dead. Mom is a walking wound, and she has wounded everyone she comes in contact with."

"Mom hates me. She never hated you. She never shot you."

"No, but she sure doesn't love me. I had enough sense to play by the rules. I acted dumb, stayed the hillbilly till I got gone and a little bit out of reach. You flaunted everything, everything that she never was, right at her. You were a sanctimonious prissy little goody two-shoes. You thought you were so great and all you did was make everyone in the family want to smack you. We were all too busy trying to save our own hides to be *improved* by you.

"And Mom's not as bad as she used to be. Mom's got outer scars, too. Dad gave them to her," I say brutally. "She's a lot better since he died. Her temper's not so bad and she's calmer. Sometimes I actually don't mind being with her."

"You stayed—"

"Somebody had to. You and Dennis—"

"We had enough sense to get away. Why didn't you? You could have made something of yourself."

"I *have* made something of myself," I say coldly. "I enjoy my job, insignificant though it may be in your eyes. I have no debts. I am not afraid in my own home, and I have done my best to be responsible to the pathetic family that I was born into. I don't want to live in Hawaii and study volcanoes. I don't want to live in Montana and be an ecological terrorist. I like Kentucky. I like the mountains. I like the quiet. I like basketball. I play Rook. I take a little vacation every so often. I am not brilliantly ecstatic, but you know what? My life is peaceful. My life is calm. And I'm sick to death of your judgment."

"Don't you think I'm sick of yours?" She picks up her glass and smacks it on the table. "Each and every one of you has persecuted me mercilessly just because I wanted something better—"

"You wanted something different. That's not the same thing. It *is not* the same thing. It wasn't what you wanted, Darlene. It was your attitude. And you still can't get that. And not one of us is as dumb as you want us to be. Nobody would have done anything except tease you about studying all the time if you hadn't been such a self-righteous little prig. Don't you understand? You caused most of your problems by being a jerk. With the attitudes floating around in that family, pathetic though they were, you were never smart enough to understand that you had to play the game to survive. Don't kid yourself about being honest to yourself. You wanted to tell us how to live. We didn't want to be told. Because nobody wanted to be like you."

"I should be like *you*? Like *Mom*?"

"No. You may be a genius in the academic world but you are an emotional idiot." I sigh, tired of having all this garbage in my head again. "I'll shut up now."

"I did the best I could at the time. You're acting like I'm still sixteen years old, like I haven't lived any, like I haven't learned a thing about being human. I am a different woman than what I was then—"

"So are we, Darlene. So are we."

To have something to do, I drain my glass again though it's long empty. When I put it down, I sigh again and look down at my hands. "I'm sorry. Sounds like we've all got a bunch of shit stored up on the inside."

"I'll say," she says, and gives a little laugh that she doesn't mean, but I appreciate the effort. "Emotionally constipated."

It's my turn to laugh a little, and I put my hand atop hers then quickly remove it. "I was scared to death the whole time I was a kid, especially those times . . . ."

She looks away.

I sigh. Maybe I know why Dennis sighs all the time—it's dealing with Darlene. "It's getting dark. I'm going back to Kivic's Motel and see if Mom's there. I don't know what else to do. Do you want to go with me?" I surprise myself by asking that.

Slowly she shakes her head. "I'll come up in the morning, early."

"Where do you live?"

"In the park. It's an arrangement made for my research. I'm being co-sponsored by the National Park Service. I'm staying near the West Thumb area."

"Why were you in Dennis's cabin?"

She looks at me. "Brenda Marlene, it's none of your business."

"All right," I say, grabbing the check. "I'll see you tomorrow."

I pay the bill, walk out into the darkness, shove my hands down into the pockets of the windbreaker, roll the tube of Harem Heartbeat around in my fingers, and find my way back to the car.

—XVII—

ANOTHER PARTIAL DENOUEMENT

The drive is uneventful; I barely have time to think about the journey because I'm thinking about something else. I seem to arrive quickly, certainly quicker than I expected.

Kivic's Motel is still there; it is still empty, but Dennis's truck is gone.

The door is unlocked. I go to my room, shut the door, then reconsider and call Othello into the room before I barricade myself in. He promptly jumps on the bed and starts rolling and twisting on the pillows. He is adorable and sweet and all that, but I have my mind on the computer.

I check my e-mail. There is nothing from Mom, not that I expect anything. It is crazy, but I have to Google Our Lady of the Poppy. I imagine explaining Googling to Dennis. "Google?" he'd say. "Ain't that what happens to your eyes when somebody squeezes your neck?" Heaven forbid that I should have to explain the concept of a search engine to him. I get a whopping six hits, so I check them all. One has nothing to do with the gold-and-purple packaged cosmetic but is the name of an all-female jazz quartet. The others are in lists on people's personal web sites as being things that these individuals want to buy or collect or are obsessed with. God, if the Internet isn't an identifiable piece of crap.

Then I go to eBay. I encounter much frustration that I will not enumerate because I use the same foul words over, unimaginatively, but I eventually am able to search for Our Lady of the Poppy Sultan's Kiss.

I find one tube for sale—the bid is already up to $243. It is being offered by one James Wiggins of Red Lodge, Montana.

Fancy that.

A cold, calculating fury consumes me. No doubt this is the same Jimmy Wiggins of Kivic's Motel. Gone not to attend a family tragedy, or even to the nearest Cougar Dive to buy his own stash of Sultan's Kiss, but to rip off my mama. Smelled a buck on my for-once-innocent Mama and reckoned that old Brenda Marlene, Poo, would surely be too dumb to figure it out. I will smoke his onion and land his pimply white ass in jail.

I leave the computer right where it is—I mean, I don't log out. I de-barricade the door, sneak down to the kitchen for weapons. I choose the standard wooden rolling pin and a steak knife small enough to slip into my jacket pocket and go to the room that I'm sure is Jimmy's. I don't take time to consider whether Dennis is in on it, or whether he's a victim too.

I don't know what I'm looking for, but I don't find it. I open every drawer, look under every piece of furniture and under the rug and under the mattress. But whatever he's hiding, it doesn't have to be here. He has this whole wreck of a motel to hide things in. While I'm at it, I explore Dennis' room, which is spartan and ascetic, then I have a flash of brilliance and hurry into the kitchen.

Where is the best place to hide something? In a place where no one will ever look for it. The garbage.

I find it wadded up inside a Celestial Seasonings tea box near the bottom of the bin: a credit card receipt signed by one Mauda Belle Simpkins. She had paid eight dollars for the case of Sultan's Kiss and six twenty-five for the Harem Heartbeat.

So this means . . . this means . . . I try to think rather than collapse, which is my initial inclination. This means that he's been back here since he did whatever it was that he did to Mom, because Mom has never been here. Jimmy was here while I was gone. He left the last message in the refrigerator, so I sling open the door but see only food. I shut the door and open the freezer. I look under and behind everything. Nothing.

Think, Brenda Marlene, think.

He probably found Mom and Dennis in the Tetons, and they got in his car with him, willingly or unwillingly. That's why my car was abandoned. Now Dennis's truck is gone. What can that mean?

Well, it can mean that Dennis is driving it. Which means that he came back here to get his truck, for whatever reason. It could mean that Jimmy brought him here to get it. It could mean he's in on it. It could mean he's a victim.

Twenty tubes to a carton, two cartons, let's say they sell for $350 per tube, times forty. That's . . . close to $15,000. Not a lot of money, but to someone who probably makes minimum wage at part-time work it's significant. I frown. What's wrong with this picture?

What's wrong with it is that I have never known Dennis to lust for money. He always worked, but he never cared about having more than enough to get by on. He could be taking advantage of an opportunity, but somehow it doesn't fit. If he wanted something, he'd be more likely to just steal it. I can't imagine him selling anything on the Internet. I don't think Dennis has any idea what people even want electricity for, and I don't think he'd know anything about online auctions.

So my brother is a victim.

Or Jimmy could have taken the truck. Why? Because Dennis stole his car? Because his car quit running? For the life of me, I can't imagine why he would come back here and get Dennis's truck.

Unless he's going to put Mom and Dennis in it and push it over the side of one of these mountain passes.

But would he kill over a few thousand dollars' worth of lipstick? How would I ever know? And why couldn't I have kept my big mouth shut? I was so eager to make Mom out to be backwards and dumb that I might have babbled her life away.

I run upstairs for my backpack and pull out the propaganda that the Park Service foists off on you when you drive through the park. I read through everything frantically and finally find a number. But now I have to shut down this fool computer and plug the phone back into the jack.

The bid is up to $485.

I call the number, praying that someone will answer. On the second ring, someone picks up, but before this person can say anything I shout, "I must have a number where I can call Dr.

Darlene Simpkins. She's living at West Thumb doing research. She's my sister, and this is a family emergency! Please!"

"Hold tight, Honey," the voice of an older woman says. "It'll take me a minute or two. There's lots of phones out here, believe it or not."

"Thank you." I'm almost hopping up and down to get her to hurry. I become aware that I'm hyperventilating and work to slow down my breathing. My fingers are already starting to draw up.

"Here you are. I don't have that name, but this is the only place assigned to a researcher." She reads a number, then says, "Want me to transfer you?"

"Oh, yes!" I cry. "Thank you so much! Thank you!"

"You're welcome, honey. Good luck."

There is a frightening silence on the line, then the ringing begins. Six rings and I hear Darlene say, "Hello?"

"Oh, Darlene. Thank God. Listen."

And to her credit, she does. I spill it all out, all about the Cougar Dives and the note in the refrigerator and the receipt in the trash and the online bid, and she doesn't say a word until I finish and inhale deeply. My hands hurt and my stomach is starting to tingle. If I keep this up, I'll pass out.

"It's not Dennis," she says quickly. "He wouldn't do that."

"I know. I believe you. What do we do?"

"I'm coming. I'll check Sylvan Pass and Craig Pass on my way. Sylvan's out of the way, so it'll take me longer. I should be there in thirty minutes."

"Don't kill yourself—"

"I know these roads. What's your number there?"

"I don't know."

"This is my cell phone number." She reels it off, but slowly enough for me to write it down. "As soon as we hang up, call me back, and we'll stay on the phone until I get there. We may lose the signal in the mountains, though. If that happens, keep calling until you get me again."

"Okay. Be careful."

"I will. I'll be there soon as I can."

"Be careful," I repeat.

"You too. Hang up and call me back," she says. "I'm ready to head out."

"I'm going to the bathroom first—"

"Okay. Bye." She hangs up, and after a second so do I.

Everything is so quiet, too quiet. Somehow even on the second floor, I can hear the refrigerator humming. I can hear the wind gust outside. I can hear Othello galloping like a horse up the stairs. I decide to listen to my breath instead—I am becoming hyperventilated enough that the tingling muscles deep in my stomach are wanting to pull me over. You can control your emotions by controlling your breath, I tell myself. I don't listen to me very well because I'm too busy listening for . . . for whatever might be getting ready to happen that I don't want to happen.

Nothing is going to happen until after I go to the bathroom, yet I crouch here, the phone still in my hand. I realize that I am afraid to get up and walk the length of the stupid hallway. A rolling pin seems but pitiful protection. What protection is anything, for that matter? Nothing is foolproof, nothing is completely bullet-proof, nothing shields every raw centimeter of vulnerability.

I release the phone and get up. I walk to the bed, lean over and squeeze the cat really, really hard. He purrs, without a worry in the world. I kiss him on his big old head, and escort myself to the bathroom with my silly weapon. It's so silly that I don't even know if it makes me feel better.

I get done in record time and rush back to the bedroom. Once inside, I push the bed in front of the door—fear certainly makes you strong. Othello doesn't move. I'm thinking I should ask Darlene what her car looks like, then I realize it doesn't matter because I don't have a window to look out of anyway. I pull a blanket over myself, and call my sister.

She answers before the first ring ends. "Yeah," she says. "Is that you?"

"Who were you expecting, the Beatles?" I snap. I'm scared, but maybe I'm starting to feel less scared, and maybe I'm starting to wish I hadn't called Darlene for help. Yet she didn't think I was stupid, so perhaps I'm not so stupid after all. "Where are you?"

"I'm on my way to one of the passes."

"Do you know what Dennis's truck looks like?"

"Of course I do."

"What about Jimmy's car?"

"I have no clue."

"Me either." I pause. "Would you know Mom if you saw her?"

She pauses, too. "I don't know—"

I butt in and describe Mom to her: the hair, the polyester pants suit, the lipstick. The attitude.

Darlene is silent for so long that I wonder if she's there. "Darlene?" I ask.

"Yeah, I'm here. Keeping my eyes peeled for a scrappy little woman. By the way, Brenda, my name's not Darlene anymore. Darlene's the name of somebody with big hair and mascara who runs the cash register at a gas station."

"And Brenda's the name of a hairdresser. So what should I call you?"

She laughs nervously. "Not Linda, either."

"Let me guess. Because Linda is a cheerleader's name."

"Nope. Because Linda is a soccer mom's name. I *legally* changed *my* name."

"So?" I say. "I've done it twice."

"You have?" she shrieks gleefully. "You really have?"

"Yeah," I chuckle. "Starflower Jade-Eagle—"

"That's what you called yourself when we were kids."

"Yeah. Ole Dandelion Poopy-Chicken. That's how come Dennis still calls me Poo. Or I guess what got him started. But I got tired of that. Too pseudo-Native American. Now I'm Cerise Cloudmist."

"That's kinda pretty," she says. "Cerise. Is that what people call you?"

"Mostly. Sometimes Rissy. Except Mom and Dennis. Of course."

"Of course. Well, I thought Darlene Simpkins sounded too much like a white-trash name."

"It *is* a white-trash name." We both laugh. This amazes me. Here we are together laughing on the phone like sisters.

"You'll laugh," she warns me.

"Probably," I agree, "but don't let that stop you."

"Anna Mary Summers," she recites quickly.

"That sounds like—"

"I know. A librarian. A Sunday school teacher. Someone who plays bridge every Thursday."

"Someone who wears an apron. So are you Annie?"

"Yeah. With one N and no E. A-N-I," she spells.

"A minimalist," I say. "You want me to call you Ani?"

"If that's okay."

"Ani Banani," I say. "What's Dennis call you?"

She sighs. "Darlene. He calls me Darlene."

Again, we both laugh. It isn't nervous laughter, either. It's laughter laughter. We're having fun. We are being sisters.

"Not Star-veeng?" I dredge up from the depths of my memory. Dennis never called anyone by their right name.

"Thank God for small blessings. So, Rissy, I'm going up the first pass."

"Should I hold my breath for you?"

"Suit yourself."

She is quiet for a few minutes. "I've got my brights on. I'm seeing nothing."

"I think that's what we want, isn't it? But shouldn't you be looking for wrecks over the side of the mountain?"

"I suppose, but I don't know how I can see that in the dark . . . and I don't know if there are any pullouts here. Maybe I'm wasting time."

"Probably. I'm sorry—"

"Don't apologize. We just need it to be daylight. I'm gonna find a place to turn around and high-tail it to Kivic's. Got anything there to eat?"

"Lots of manly junk food. We can eat what I've not already consumed."

"Dennis doesn't eat civilized food," she says. "Do you?"

"Of course," I say. "As highly processed and as artificially flavored as possible. Deep fried is a plus. Don't tell me you live on watercress and pineapple."

"Nope. Field scientists the world over subsist on peanut butter sandwiches and beer. Sometimes I substitute tahini."

"Yuck," I say. "It's bitter and it makes you poop."

Darlene laughs, but suddenly I'm not listening to what she's saying.

I'm listening to something else.

I'm listening to a vehicle in the parking area.

I'm dead meat. Because my car is in the parking area, too. My presence here won't be a secret to anybody. I'm advertised.

I interrupt Darlene. Ani. "Somebody's here. I have to go and see."

"What do you mean?"

"I mean I hear a car pulling into the parking area. I have to go see who it is. I'm in the room with the fake window and I can't see out."

"Fake window?"

"I'll explain later." Stupid Darlene. "But I need to know who's here. Hold on."

"Brenda—"

But by that time I'm across the room and starting to un-barricade the door. I have really barricaded myself in quite effectively. I don't bother to consider that perhaps I should stay here and let the newcomer find me, let him have the joy of moving all the furniture and rubbish that I've piled against the door. But I'm too nosy. I have to see.

By the time I get out in the hallway and listen, I'm hearing footsteps in the kitchen. Othello has said, "Mrrnk!" and raced down the hall and stairs. I slide my shoes off and sneak to the stairwell.

"Poo!" I hear Dennis call. "Where are you, Poo?"

I listen hard. I listen hard enough that I'm sure he's alone before I put my shoes on and go down the stairs.

—XVIII—

FINDING MOM

"Just a minute!" I yell, and run back up the stairs. I grab the phone, out of breath.

"It's Dennis," I gasp. "He's by himself. I'm gonna hang up."

"Okay. I'll be there in fifteen minutes." I don't know if she says anything else because I've crashed the phone down.

"Dennis!" I scream. "Is Mom with you?"

"Nope!" he hollers as I barrel into the kitchen. "You mean she ain't here with you? Poo, what's wrong? Is Mom okay?"

"You didn't leave her with Jimmy, did you?"

"Yeah. He—"

"Christ, you bonehead. He's just after her lipstick!"

"Her lipstick! Poo, you're clean out of your head."

"Then tell me why James Wiggins of Red Lodge is selling one of Mom's lipsticks on eBay?"

"What's eBay? Some kind of computer foolishness?"

"Yeah—"

"That screwy Jimmy, messin' with all that computer garbage. All that virtual shit. I keep telling him that *virtual* don't mean anything but *almost*. Who wants an *almost* anything?"

"Listen. This is the lipstick that Mom bought at Cougar Dive that she was so proud of. I figure at online auction prices she's got at least $15,000 worth of lipstick, probably more. I found the receipt from where she bought those in the garbage can right over there." I point. "She's never been here. And that makes me very, very frightened."

Dennis is white. He is staring at me with his mouth open.

"Sit down! Dennis, sit down before you faint!" I grab hold of one of his mammoth arms and ease him down into one of those Formica kitchen chairs.

"I'm gonna puke," he whispers.

"Put your head down." As he leans over his knees, I run cold water on a dishrag and then dab it across his forehead.

"He'll kill her," I hear him say. "He's done time. He ain't been out long."

"Then suck it up. There's no time for you to be sick," I snap. "When was the last time you saw her?"

"Taggart Lake," he croaks, then looks up at me. "Is that where you found your car?"

I nod.

"We was mad at you, Poo—"

"I was ready to kill both of you, too. Tell me what happened."

"We run into him at Taggart Lake. We was trying to have a picnic in the parking lot. She kept bleating about how much she wanted to pet a wapiti and whether I knowed where Harrison Ford lived. Who's Harrison Ford?"

"Indiana Jones."

"Who?"

"It doesn't matter. So he showed up at your picnic?"

"Yeah. He said he'd been to the hotel looking for us. You and your ignorant name, Cerise. Piece of cake to call all the budget hotels in Jackson and ask for Cerise Cloudmist. But he said . . . he said that her sister had called at Kivic's and that there was an emergency."

"That asshole. He left a note that somebody in his family had crashed into a floodwall and that he was going home for a family emergency. I even felt sorry for him."

Dennis looks more like himself now. "We both got in his car and left yours. Like I said, I was mad at you, Poo, mad as hell. There's a store that's got a couple of phones . . . There ain't none here."

"You moron, why did you believe Mom's sister called if there's no phone? How do you think he gets online? He's gotta have a phone jack to plug his damn computer into to get on the Internet. There's a jack in my room and a phone under the bed."

"But the phone company—"

"Damn it, Dennis! You plug phones in yourself now. You buy your own phone and plug it into the jack. It takes a tenth of a second!" I sigh. "So he took you guys to this store."

"Yeah. It wasn't that far from here as the crow flies, so I cut across the mountain to come and pick up my truck. But when I went back to meet up with them, they was gone."

He looks at me as though I'm able to do something.

"He needs $15,000?"

Dennis shrugs. "Don't know that need has much to do with wanting money. Do I think he'd be a criminal for it? I sure do."

I wait a few seconds, but he doesn't explain.

I ask softly, "Where would he take her? Do you have any ideas?"

Dennis sighs and looks out the window—which he can actually do because the window in this room is real.

"Come on, you bonehead!" I exclaim. "You've got to have some kind of clue!"

"He won't kill her," he begins. I don't know whether he's changing his mind or whether he's trying to convince himself.

"He damn well better not," I retort. "I want her. I want her here with me. I want her safe, and I want her stupid lipstick, and I want to go home."

"Okay," he says, getting up. "Let's go."

"We can't go anywhere yet. Darlene's not here."

He stares at me with his mouth open, like I've burped out a big whooshing flame or spit up a mouthful of silver dollars. So I stare right back at him. He shuts his mouth and swallows.

"Time's a-wastin', Cowboy," I say.

"Darlene?" he croaks.

"Yeah," I say. "Darlene. Ani. Our sister. We met. We ate together. We called a truce. Shall I put it into Latin?"

I am really impressed with myself that I can make an allusion to Julius Caesar, but it is lost on Dennis. He just continues gawping at me as though I've really done something. Like blow a beagle puppy out of my nose.

"Latin?" he asks. He looks as confused as the beagle puppy I just blew out of my nose. It's a cute little thing, more black than white.

"Darlene is coming here—"

"What for? How'd you meet her?"

I shrug. "I went up to your Cooke City resort cabin looking for Mom. I found Darlene under a box in the front room."

"What was she doing under a box?"

"She wouldn't tell me anything except she was looking for you. I guess she's observed that you regularly hide out beneath dirty old boxes. It takes all kinds." I look at him—he is still dumbfounded. "I want some coffee before we go back out. Sit back down and get a grip on yourself."

Slowly he sits down, looking perhaps a bit less dazed, but still like someone has whapped him in the head with a two-by-four.

"You say there's a phone here. Have you been talking to Darlene?"

"Yep."

"Then call her back," he says decisively. "We need to go. Tell her to meet us there."

"Where?" I say, then wince at my unconscious echo of my mother's suddenly endearing question.

"Red Lodge," he says, standing up. "Time's a-wastin'. Get a move on."

I get a move on.

—XIX—

RED LODGE

It occurs to me as we are speeding through the darkness to wonder what Dennis knows about this Jimmy Wiggins's past and how the two of them met, and especially what led to Dennis moving in to Uncle Wiggins' Kivic's Motel, if that wasn't a lie, too, but I don't ask. We ride in silence. Dennis is driving my car—it's smaller and quieter, and will be easier to camouflage once we get there. He is driving very fast, tight-lipped and white-knuckled. He has to know something terrible, something so frightening, so potentially dangerous, that he can't verbalize it. I can't believe that he's sparing me.

Darlene will meet us there. She said a very bad word when I called her, because it would have been better for her to have gone another way if we're meeting at Red Lodge and she was getting low on gas. If that isn't the moral of the story—there's another road we could have taken and things would have been better. "Things"—relationships, money, peace of mind, convenience, self-acceptance. Life. And the thin line upon which we wobble seems nearly invisible now—there's nothing to balance upon. I just hope my free-fall etches a pattern of beauty on the dark void, and that the bones I break when I hit the bottom will be insignificant. Or that I find some kind of grace, some kind of faith, to keep tracking my soles on that thin line that's still there even though I can't see it or feel it.

I am somewhere in Montana, or perhaps Wyoming, in the dark. I realize that I will never see the land, the places, the cartography we are driving through, and that knowledge makes me unexpectedly melancholy. I will never know what Red Lodge,

Montana, looks like. The sky is so dark that it's invisible and completely unknowable, and it's as corny and as clichéd as a soap opera, but there's a sweet light that's glowing somewhere inside me, not in my heart or in my brain but somewhere in the muscular depths behind my belly button. It is in whatever connects me to the universe, where the unseen string is attached that pulls me along.

We are there too soon, and not soon enough.

"I'll take the back way in," he says, making a sharp left into a wide and relatively stable unpaved road. He turns off the headlights. I keep my mouth shut to keep the behind-my-belly-button light inside me.

Before long I can make out something, some buildings lit by security lights. And I swear that I can see . . . I squint to try to clarify the vision, and it really is. I shake my head and I know I'm going to laugh like some hysterical dimwit. Because I see . . . .

"A golf course!" I shriek. "You're a guard at a frigging country club!"

"It's not a country club—"

"I thought you worked at, like, a sawmill or, I don't know, some he-man hunting outdoorsman outfit. You guard duffers and champagne-sniffing bubbleheads!"

"It's not a country club," he repeats. "It's . . . it's . . . ."

I try to control my snickering before I get the hiccups. I sound like I'm choking. "It's a country club!" I snort.

"It's a country club," he repeats, breaking into a grin. "It *is* a frigging country club. And I don't just nightwatch there. Honey, I own it."

Now it's my turn to stare at him. And I do stare.

"Shut your mouth, Poo. You'll catch flies."

"You own a country club? Mr. Mountain Man Environmental Terrorist? You own a country club?"

"Know thine enemy," he grins. "Just think of it as a backwards church." But before I can ask him to explain, he says, "Later. I got to think now."

I don't say, "And you can't talk and think at the same time," because I've remembered to be scared again. He pulls my car to a stop beside a little bitty something that looks like a changing room for a swimming pool, but of course there's no pool.

Dennis stops me when I begin to open the door—he puts his big paw over my wrist. He rolls down the window and listens.

I don't hear anything. I just feel the cold air—God, it's cold. I consciously clench my teeth to keep them from chattering. No, it's not that cold, but . . . you know.

I still don't hear anything, but Dennis whispers, "Darlene."

Then she's at the side of the car. She reaches in and squeezes Dennis' shoulder. "Glad you're okay, big guy," she whispers. "You okay, Poo?"

I nod. Despite the seriousness of the situation, we all feel happy. A miracle has happened. A miracle out here in this completely godforsaken place. We are together again, after nearly a quarter of a century. We three Simpkins siblings are together, and we like each other. For the first time in our lives, we are on the same side. We don't even look related anymore, but for the first time in our lives we are.

Dennis is asking Darlene where she's parked and she's telling him something—I don't pay attention.

"Is he here?" I ask, too loudly.

"That's the question, ain't it?" Dennis says. "Let's go."

I don't know where we're going, but I get out of the car, close the door quietly, and trail along with them in the dark. I can only think about foolish things, like where Dennis got the money to buy this place. He had to be pulling my leg. No way can a white trash Simpkins own a country club, even in Montana. He's got to be fibbing again.

But we're quiet now, so quiet that I have to think about it to even hear our own six footsteps. Sneaky mountain folk, that's us. Then suddenly, I'm scared again. Mom could be out here somewhere, tied up and cold, hurt. Maybe more than hurt. I'll string up that damn Wiggins and peel the skin off his body while he's still alive. Bet he'll squall. I shiver—I'm making myself sick. I hate being squeamish.

We walk around the little building and around another. At the back of the next, Dennis tries the door. It's locked. He fishes in his pocket for a key, and in the darkness has a heck of a time fitting it into the lock. I'm colder than ever standing still.

Finally we pass through the door. He leaves it unlocked. There's a big bang—Darlene has walked into a bucket or a big can. She cringes. So much for stealth.

"Might as well turn on the light," I grouch. Dennis elbows me in the ribs.

"A man can't hear hisself think," he hisses.

"Neither can a woman," Darlene sasses right back at him.

"You two wait right here—"

"No!" we both whisper forcefully.

We hold hands and move along in the darkness behind Dennis. It seems like a long time passes, even though I know logically that it's probably no more than a couple of minutes at the most. I reach a place where I'm aware of some light just around a corner to the right, enough light that I can now see my siblings, and I wonder if I look as scared and as freaky as they do. Knowing me, I look about twenty times worse.

Dennis puts a finger to his lips, and we are still. I listen so hard that I forget to breathe, which for me is never a good thing. He mouths, "Stay here!" and this time neither of us argues with him. What a difference a little light makes. Darlene and I keep our hands clasped together. We watch him turn the corner, then walk into another room. He turns on a light, and we both wince with the brightness of it.

"Anybody here?" he hollers.

There's an answering *bang*! Metallic, not like a gun.

More racket in the room Dennis is in, then I hear a familiar bleat. "Dennis! My boy! Honey, is that you?"

I squeeze Darlene's little hand. "It's her," I whisper, ready to cry.

"It's all right now, Mom," I hear him say, his voice echoing weirdly. "What're you doing inside that old refrigerator?"

"I ain't in here for my health, that's for sure. Get me out of here. I'm about froze to death. I can't feel nothing in my legs."

"Here, I'm gonna pick you up—"

Mom squalls, "Careful, you big lummox!"

"You're just stiff from sitting for so long. Grab hold of my neck, Mommy."

She makes a squawking sound and mumbles, "You sure

are a smart boy. How'd you know to look for me in here?"

"Poo figured it out. Poo told me."

"You're lying, sure as I'm alive. Brenda Marlene don't have the sense God give a turnip."

I nudge Darlene—someone's coming down the hallway from the other direction. It's Jimmy Wiggins, and he has a gun.

He slides into the room Dennis and Mom are in. "What a touching scene!" he exclaims in his skinny voice. "Put her back in that refrigerator. Now."

"That's the jackass—" Mom begins.

"Won't do it. You'll have to kill me first," Dennis says.

Darlene has slipped away from me, and I follow her down the hall. She dashes through the doorway, a tiny gun in her hand.

"Drop it!" she yells.

I'm right behind her, gaping goggle-eyed at her, just like everyone else is. Dennis is holding Mom up in his arms like she's a baby or a damsel in distress. Jimmy is holding a big black pistol pointed at Mom, and staring at Darlene with his mouth open.

"Drop it!" Darlene repeats. When Jimmy doesn't move, she fires into the floor. He jumps and Dennis mutters, "Christ!"

"I'm not telling you again," my sister says.

He lowers the gun.

"Put it on that table," Darlene says, never taking her gun or her eyes away from him. "Then go stand by the stove, with your hands in the air. Now."

To my utter amazement, he does. Darlene keeps the gun aimed straight at his gut.

"If you think I'm going to congratulate you, think again," Darlene says slowly. "I'm still going to shoot you."

Before anyone can blink or utter a syllable, she shoots again, aiming at his left foot.

Jimmy screams. Mom starts yelling, "Darlene! Oh, my God, it's Darlene!" and I break out in a cold sweat. Before I can say that I'm going to faint, even though Jimmy's just standing there looking confused and I don't see any blood, my knees buckle and I hit the floor.

—XX—

THE END

Mom can't stop talking about Darlene, about how little and pretty she is, how brave she is and what a good shot she is. She missed on purpose, she told us. Hah! The little genius lost her nerve at the last minute and shot into the floor again. What a weenie. At least there wasn't anything disgusting to clean up.

It is the next day, and the four of us are having a farewell meal in the Moose Lick Cafe. We have splurged on a real meal instead of the ubiquitous Teddyburgers, magnificent though they are. Part of this is occasioned by the fact that it is just after seven in the morning, so we've ordered from the breakfast menu. We're all eating the Cholesterol Special: scrambled eggs, fried potatoes, sausage, biscuits and gravy, and close to two gallons of coffee as black as old motor oil. It's a meal fit for a king, queen, and all the royal progeny.

Generally we are happy with each other. I am especially happy because as soon as this meal is over, Mom and I will start the long haul back to Kentucky. The sun shines bright on my old Kentucky home. It probably has never shined this brightly before.

"I couldn't believe it when you shot at that feller," Mom says to Darlene. "I figured you was gonna shoot me. If I was you, that's what I'd have done—I'd a shot myself."

"I had no intention of shooting myself," Darlene says, with a funny little laugh.

"Now, Linda Darlene, if you're sitting there expecting me to apologize for the past, you can just keep on waiting. Whatever

I did was the best I could do at the time, so I offer no apologies for it."

"Likewise I offer no apologies for doing my best," the professor begins, but Dennis chooses this opportunity to burp loudly, before Mom and Darlene start bickering and kicking one another under the table. He hollers for more coffee.

"You was raised better than that," Mom begins.

"No, I wasn't," Dennis butts in. "I was raised like I lived in a barn."

Mom laughs.

"There's something I just have to ask you," I say to Dennis. "There's no way on God's green earth that you own that country club."

We look at each other a long moment. "That ain't a question, Poo," he says.

"Do you own that country club, Dennis Simpkins?" I ask.

"Tell me where it was."

"Why, the one where—Red Lodge, Montana."

"There's no country club in Red Lodge, Montana."

"You idiot dunce," I say. "Where in the hell were we then?"

Darlene laughs again.

"It sure wasn't Red Lodge." Dennis laughs. "I don't hardly think it was even Montana."

"I don't know what's so funny—"

"I do," Mom interrupts. "They lied to you about where they took you, and now they think it's funny that you was dumb enough to believe them. Brenda Marlene ain't playing with a full deck," she says pointedly to Dennis, as Darlene cackles again, "but generally she's got a good heart and does the best she can. She's the only one of you who's ever done diddly for her poor old mother. The both of you put together ain't worth her little fingernail." I stare at her with my jaws hanging open. "Don't you go getting the big head," she says to me.

"Okay, Mom," I say, refusing to be speechless or overcome in front of my siblings, though this is the nicest thing Mom's ever said to me in her entire life, "where did that boy take you?"

"There is no doubt in my mind," says my mother, adopting

her pitiful little-old-lady tone of voice again, "that I was south of Canada and north of Mexico. Probably closer to Canada, because I'm always heading straight ahead. And that's north."

Darlene stares at her, but Dennis has heard this before. "Mommy—"

"And west of the Mississippi. Will we get across it today, Brenda?"

"Not unless we get in an airplane. Tomorrow, if we're lucky."

"Tomorrow if we're lucky," she repeats. Then she turns to Darlene. "Did I give you one of my lipsticks? That Sultan's Kiss would really look good on you with your fair complexion."

"Yes. One of each. I'll probably keep them as souvenirs." They smile nicely at one another.

"Not me," I declare loudly. "I'm gonna use mine up and go on to bigger and better things."

"You ain't never wore lipstick in your life, Brenda girl. Not that I didn't try to teach you to take care of your looks. You never know who might be watching."

"I don't care who might be watching. I please myself, and everybody else can go to hell in a bucket."

"I don't think you please yourself, Poo—" Dennis begins.

"E, S, and D," I tell him, shorthand for one of our childhood insults, like we ever needed to talk our way around ugly language in our family.

"Can't make me," Dennis says.

"You childern shut up," Mom says. "I'm about to get the headache." She pauses. "But last night I dreamed that the President passed a law that made it mandatory for every single woman over the age of fifty-eight to stop at every single Cougar Dive that was on the roads they were traveling. And they also made it a law that they had to have one every two miles along the road if the road had a good passing lane. If they didn't have a good passing lane, they only had to have one every three point seven miles."

"Nope," I say emphatically. "Absolutely not. No way hoe-zay."

"Brenda Marlene—"

"Not if you buy me fries and a shake at every McDonald's on the way home. Not even if you swipe my fries in ketchup and feed them to me with your own little fingers."

"What are you talking about?" Darlene asks. "I want another biscuit."

"You always eat that much?" Mom says. "Here. I don't want this one. But be careful not to eat too much bread or it'll turn to glue inside you and plug up your bowels."

I roll my eyes. "She's telling me that she wants to stop at all the Cougar Dives on the way home. You see what having all that lipstick got you into," I scold her.

"It got me rich," she says. "Rich as thieves. I need to go to the little girls' room." She looks at me expectantly.

"You know where it is," I tell her.

"I'll go with you, Mom," Darlene says.

"I hope you behave yourself better than your sister. When we went in there before she was always trying to peep into the men's stall."

I roll my eyes again. Sometime they're going to stick up there, and I'll have to walk around with my nose jammed into my ribcage to be able to see anything.

They leave. Dennis and I look at each other. "It's been good, ain't it?" he says at last, but he doesn't quite smile.

"Yeah," I say. "It's been something." I don't smile, either.

"But don't let's do it again any time soon."

They come back to the table. Mom is ready.

"I was trying to tell your sister about directions, but she won't listen to nothing. I told her we're headed north."

"East."

"Sideways," Mom scoffs.

I shake my head. "Home," I say. "Home."